A FISTFUL OF MUSTARD SEEDS

a collection of short stories

E. SANTHOSH KUMAR

Translated from Malayalam by
P.N. VENUGOPAL

THORNBIRD
NIYOGI
BOOKS

Published by
NIYOGI BOOKS
Block D, Building No. 77,
Okhla Industrial Area, Phase-I,
New Delhi-110 020, INDIA
Tel: 91-11-26816301, 26818960
Email: niyogibooks@gmail.com
Website: www.niyogibooksindia.com

Editor: K.E. Priyamvada
Design: Shashi Bhushan Prasad

ISBN: 978-93-89136-19-7
Publication: 2019

Printed at: Niyogi Offset Pvt. Ltd., New Delhi, India

Contents

Introduction

Building our little worlds brick by brick

These 12 stories, written and published in Malayalam over a period of almost two decades, represent different phases in my writing career spanning a quarter of a century now. I have published more than 60 stories during this period, apart from writing one novel and a few novellas. In some of these years, especially in the initial ones, I could be prolific enough to produce more than six works a year, but there were lean patches as well, when I could not write even a single story for months together. That explains why the themes are drastically different from one another, even though there can be a few undercurrents that connect them like a blood stream. Again the diversity is always welcome, for working on a story is like working on a life, a set of characters around the geography where they live and a whole new world altogether. Writers create new worlds and new people. While writing stories at least, they do play God, in their little way.

Towards the last years of the 1990s, Malayalam fiction, especially short stories, witnessed the emergence of many writers possessing different narratives, themes and techniques. Some of these writers were young, starting to get published after being rejected by the mainstream media for quite long. It is really refreshing to listen to new voices, in any language, any time, because the new writers bring new worlds with them.

And still some of these writers of the 1990s were, in fact, not new writers at all but those who were coming back to writing after many years of self-inflicted silence. This silence, at least in their case, was not a bane, but a blessing that helped them find their own voices in a renewed ambience. This resurgence of these seasoned writers triggered a volley of young talent to focus more seriously on their works. Thus emerged a new phase in Malayalam fiction in the new millennium, to which, in all modesty, I believe I belong.

Literature in Malayalam, can never avoid political undertones—it is our destiny—essentially because we are a politically charged society. Except for some outdated romantic works, which are also served in the name of fiction, almost all the literature here hovers around politics, especially Left politics. Some are unfortunately sheer propaganda, as is the vogue in Left literary circles, but some do really depict the subtle politics of the time, like good literature always does. And the 1990s were the worst time for the Left, as the artificially built walls collapsed fast and the regimes that were built inside such walls collapsed even faster. The writings in the 1990s caught the pain, shock, trauma and even surprise of the unprecedented happenings from all around the world. The intelligentsia failed to provide the answers or when they tried to do so, they were unable to comprehend the real questions. So fiction thrived because only fiction can raise questions, unmindful of whether answers are really coming or not.

Another revolution was also happening the same time, the Information one, which toppled a few other power centres, like never before in human history. So the stories of these times, cannot escape from the politics of both these events.

This book is the result of the constant motivation of our publisher, Niyogi Books. I have had the privilege of having published my novel in translation by them in 2015 (*Island of Lost Shadows*). A big thank you to Team Niyogi for their encouragement. Priyamvada, our editor, has been a great support, for being sharp in her reading and for her wonderful suggestions. The book would not have been what it is, but for her insights.

A translated work is the product of two people, the author and the translator. So it may be inappropriate to thank a co-author, and since we have been working together for long. But I owe my friend P.N. Venugopal for his dedication and perseverance, for these translations also span over two decades. Thank you reposing your trust in my stories and in me.

Now it's over to you, dear readers. These 12 stories; 12 different worlds.

Warm regards,
E. Santhosh Kumar

Hills, Stars

There were three houses on the hill slope and there were four or five children in these three houses. Their parents would go early in the morning to their places of work in the small town at the foot of the hills. The children were left to themselves till their parents returned. They went to school through the forest lanes. Rabbits and birds waited in expectation for them. Old trees, standing tall, bowed their branches affectionately, as the children drew near. Gurgling streams provided them company for some distance. While returning, from afar, the children could see the three houses along the slopes lost in deep thought, like wise men. In the sky behind, three pale stars shone, lighting the way.

~

In the twilight, they played games in the courtyard. Thief and police, tiger and ox, marbles, head ball and many other games.

A narrow road starting from the distant mountains went down in front of the three houses. Trucks laden with fruits and vegetables and bamboo and wooden logs rushed down to the town early in the morning. Late in the night, they would groan their way back up the mountain. Buses also went up and down the road, once in a while. A long whistle would mean that a bus is stopping there. There will be passengers to get in or get down. But they would wait for some more time with the engine chugging and shivering, as if struggling to retrieve something from memory. The boys would stop their games and watch the buses. They were all painted green, red and blue. There was always something unendingly new in the bus scenes. Different kinds of people, the elderly, small babies, multi-coloured dresses, cane baskets on the top of the bus; after some time the conductor would blow his whistle twice. That was the signal that the bus was leaving. The kids would then wave at the passengers. Some of them would gaze at them with curiosity, some of them would wave back. The kids would return to their games.

Recently, one of the kids had got hold of a whistle of the same kind, from his school. The whistle changed their games absolutely. He blew a long blast on the whistle, hiding behind the flowering shrubs in front of the house. The trucks winding down the slope were his target. Trucks can also be stopped by blowing a whistle, he had told his friends. There was tough competition among them just to touch the whistle that could bring the large vehicles to a halt with its magical sound. They waited with great anticipation for the trucks that would appear only at great intervals. Their bodies trembled like the heart of baby birds, when they heard the sound of the trucks from far off. But despite all of them trying alternately, not one lorry stopped. Let alone stopping, they did not even reduce their speed. They got fed up with the game within a couple of days. No one wanted the whistle anymore. With whom is it now? Who cares!

Sometime later, the naughtier among them, came up with a new trick on his own. He would bring 10 and 20 paise coins and keep them on the road. If he was lucky, the wheel of the truck would go rolling over the coin. That was the miracle! Once the truck wheel rolled over, it was a sight! It would get elongated to the size of a little papad.

The numbers and letters would get elongated and the Ashoka pillar and the grains would get flattened like those made for the land of ghosts. They would display it in front of their schoolmates, tempt them and would also exchange them for a lens that could burn cotton and paper, or for a toy binoculars or toy gun. In course of time, those coins became a common feature in the school. Anyone could get it if required. At the most a magnolia flower – that was the price of a coin. The craze for it had come to an end. A rainy season and a winter passed by. Thunder and lightning flowered in the skies above the mountains. The leaves of the trees reddened, they became yellow and eventually fell off.

~

Summer vacation. Heat spread its net all around. Wildfire could be seen in the distant mountains in the night. The fire, which spread apparently in a single file, seemed to be showing the way to the god's abode on the top of the hill. But there was nothing during the day. The winds, which commenced from the pockets of tall trees, stayed afloat for a little while, blocked by the houses on the mountain slopes, then flew to the lower regions, swinging their invisible wings.

On an afternoon, the naughty boy came up with another trick. They were playing in the courtyard of the lowest house on the hill slope. He had a fairly large paper packet with him. They were taken aback when he opened the packet and showed them the contents. Broken glass pieces! They seemed to be the pieces of a heavy bottle. The kids said, 'No dear. No playing with glass pieces. Hands will get cut.' He merely smiled in response. Then he picked up each piece and examined it minutely. He patted the sharpest edges with affection. Kids surrounded him. They felt that there was something miraculous hidden inside the glass pieces. There was a lesson to be taught to the truck drivers who do not stop on hearing the whistle. He looked at the friends around and declared, 'You watch. Their pride has to be shown its place'.

'You plan to throw glass pieces at them? Is this your programme? We are frightened.'

'I'm not throwing any glass at them.' He smiled as if it was a trifle. 'Don't be afraid. Stand behind this bush and watch. I'll do the rest of it.'

They saw him going to the road with that packet. On reaching the road he looked in the direction of the mountains. They were coming down from that direction. Then he turned and looked at the valley. The scalding road went downhill like a loner. There were no sounds of any vehicles climbing up. He picked up a piece from the packet and kept it on the road. Its sharp tip jutted out. The glass piece was glinting in the sunlight. He took a good look all around and then retreated to the courtyard.

'Great! Fabulous idea!' the children cheered.

'Ssssss … don't make noise.' He restrained them. The children lowered themselves behind the line of bushes. Is there any sound whirring up from either the top or the bottom of the mountain? They sharpened their ears.

~

After some time a truck came from the foot of the hill. The children watched it slowly going up with baited breath. Nothing happened. They could see the glitter of the glass piece even after the lorry passed by.

'So this is your latest invention!' The children laughed with disappointment. 'Will stop the truck! Oaf!'

'Wait. Don't start ridiculing me. Perhaps that driver saw it and changed track.'

He walked up to the road. He repositioned the glass piece to the center of the road. Now it will be difficult to deviate and avoid it. He surveyed the surroundings and joined his friends.

This time the truck came from the top of the hill. Huge logs with green moss were jutting out in a haphazard way. The truck seemed to be moving quite fast. The fat driver was looking to the sides more than necessary. And because of this, the kids were certain that he would not notice the glass piece; the big tyres will get trapped and will lose air. If it happens so, will the fatty behind the wheels detect the trick? The kids were frightened seeing the bulk of the driver. May this truck miss the glass, only the next vehicle's tyre burst, they wished. Perhaps the driver of that truck will not be this sturdy. Good luck or bad luck, nothing happened to this one too. The truck flashed past them without even an inkling of what was set for it.

'Here, your glass has become a paste,' one of them pointed out. He was right. That piece which had sharp points had been shattered and had become mere dust particles spread over the road. They all cheered after a few minutes. 'Enough is enough. We will play something else. If we get a ball and a flat piece of wood, there is a game called cricket. I'll show you how to play.'

'Wait. This has to be decided either way,' he said. 'We will try once more.' Opening his paper packet, he selected a sturdy piece and walked to the road. Near the spot where the earlier one had been crushed, he fixed the new one with the sharp tip pointed upwards. A motorcycle passed by, as he was walking back. He pretended to be looking for something, so as to avoid suspicion.

No vehicles came by for quite sometime. It was a route with meagre traffic. It was noon. With only waiting and nothing happening, the children's interest had evaporated. They spread out over the courtyard and the side boundaries, where there were bushes, and started playing cops and robbers. Only the glass kid, who had not given up hope as yet, waited near the road. He could hear the shouts of those playing police and thief. All the trucks that came infrequently, passed by on the opposite side of the glass trap. The sun became mild and the wind coming down from the mountain was becoming cool. A red bus coming from the valley stopped in front of the house, announcing that it was four o'clock and dropped off two women. Nothing was happening. The child with the glass piece also got fed up. He too went away to the rear of the house to join others. They made him a robber. The cops and robbers game became more exciting. Everyone forgot about stopping the vehicles with the glass trick.

The sun was getting cooler.

Suddenly there was a big sound from the road. Like a cracker going off. The hide-and-seek players got frightened at first. Then they came running. A fairly large but old car was on the road, leaning to one side. 'See! Trapped!' The glass kid's shouts were somewhat loud. He was afraid that someone may have heard it. Everyone was apprehensive after the initial excitement. The other kids went and hid behind the bushes.

~

The car was leaning towards the side of the tyre that had been punctured. It had a dirty white complexion, similar to fading memories. The car was facing in the direction of the town. The children were looking at the car intently from their hideouts. No one came out of the car for quite some time. After some time they saw a very old man opening the front door and getting out. He walked very slowly towards the burst tyre. He walked with a slight stoop, as he was taller than usual. After standing there for some time, he started looking around. When that gaze came towards the sides of the house, the children who became frightened ran away. Only the boy who had fixed the glass piece on the road remained there. Even as a mysterious delight was filling the mind, he couldn't move from there.

Tree-tops swayed in the wind. Sunlight faded. The street was deserted. Only that man and his damaged car were left. The boy kept his eyes pinned on him from behind the thicket. Now he came to the back of the car and opened the back door with some difficulty. When the door was opened the boy saw a lady lying on the seat.

'What a spot to get a puncture!' The boy heard him cursing. 'What will we do now? There is still another 10 to 15 kilometers to go. Chhe..! Just as your mind! Everything going wrong.'

Despite that man saying all this, the woman continued to lie on the seat. She did not even raise her head to look at the situation. He continued to murmur for some more time. One or two trucks passed them by and went uphill. He opened the boot after closing the back door. Since the car was pretty old, a groaning sound emerged whenever he opened the doors. The boy saw him bending down and shaking and pulling at something.

After trying hard for sometime, he managed to pull out a tyre from the boot. And as a result of the exertion, he started panting badly. Poor man, the kid thought. He felt that he should not have done what he did, for the first time. He sweated in spite of the cool breeze. A huge truck sped down the road blocking his vision. Wild vines were hanging down from the bags stacked in the truck. He saw the old man sitting down near the boot with bent head, quite exhausted, even after the truck had sped away.

He came out of the cover of the green leaves and slowly walked towards the man.

~

He stood near him for a couple of minutes. Then asked, 'Shall I join you?'

Only then did the man raise his head. His face was wrinkled. The remaining hair had gone grey.

'Tyre burst,' he said with frustration.

'Can't you change the tyre?' He pointed to the tyre lying near the old man. There was a shadow of anguish in his voice.

'No. I cannot raise the jack or roll the wheel back.' He looked at the kid and smiled weakly, 'I am old, no?'

'I'll also join you,' he said again.

'But you are only a child.' His smile was pale. 'You don't have the strength to lift these things. Is there anyone else in your home?'

'No, all of them have gone for work.'

'It's okay.' He got up and said, 'We can try to stop one of the vehicles by hand signal.'

'None of them will stop here.' He thought of the trucks that did not stop even at the sound of a whistle.

'Let's see,' he turned to the road and said, without being loud.

He showed his hand at the trucks and jeeps that passed by infrequently. But it was like the kid had said. No vehicle stopped there. Most of them did not even mind them. A few of them slowed down and gave them a glance, but then sped away, as if nothing untoward had happened.

'Who is it inside?' The kid looked into the car and asked.

'What a trap I'm in!' The old man exclaimed. He turned towards the kid. 'That is my wife. I am taking her to the hospital.'

'What happened?'

'She is sick. Very sick. That is what it is.'

'What will you do now?'

'What to do! Should take her to the hospital, one way or other.' He was panting.

The boy became sad. Not knowing what to say, he gaped at the old man.

'Her breathlessness got worse by noon.' He tried to elaborate. 'We have a driver. But the devil won't be available when there is a need. What to do! I drove. I don't drive these days.'

'It is not that,' the boy said. But he stopped midway.

'But who thought about such a trap!' He cursed himself.

They continued their signalling at all incoming vehicles. The boy had now moved almost to the centre of the road.

'No need to go to that extent, child. Some drivers do not bother about such things.'

Now it was almost twilight. The ambient light had dimmed.

It saddened the boy that the poor woman was lying sick in the car all this while. He peered into the car occasionally. She was lying as she was. The old man was still looking into the distance for vehicles.

Then a truck came and stopped close to them.

~

The boy saw the picture of a ghost hanging from the front of the truck towards the bottom. Its tongue was trickling blood.

The truck driver and his helper got the tyre changed. Both of them had a good physique. Both of them had red towels wrapped around their heads. They took very little time for the whole task. They handled the task as easily as if it were a toy car.

The old man offered them money, but they did not accept it. 'That we will take another time,' they said and sped away in their truck. The child did not understand what they meant by another time. Is it when the tyre burst next time? When will it be?

'Its quite late,' the old man said. 'Let me leave quickly. Must reach there before it gets dark.' He started the car.

'Hey child, what shall I give you?' He looked at him in doubt. 'Money for chocolate?'

'No,' he said. 'As such, I did not do anything.' He stole a glance at the courtyard as he said this. 'Are there any of his friends there? Will they come out with the truth?' he thought to himself.

After the car turned and went down and out of sight, he took out the paper packet containing the glass pieces and threw it away angrily across the road to the other side.

He could hear the uproar of his friends from behind the house.

~

His father's job was repairing huge machines of the factory in the town. Machines that were very tall and had wheels that were always rotating with a terrible sound. His hands were rough because of his nursing of the machines. He always smelled of oil and grease. The khaki dress, which would be in a packet that he brought with him, when he came home in the evening, also had the same smell. His mother worked in a textile shop in the same town. Her job was to stitch pictures on the ready-made dresses. When she returned from work, there would be crumbs of threads of various colours sticking on to her clothes.

Together they went to the town and returned. They would talk continuously while preparing dinner in the night. It was always about their respective work floors, the news from there and their problems. This will continue while eating and also for some more time after that. He would go to sleep hearing those stories. Sometimes in his sleep machines would rotate in circles on huge wheels. Or birds with embroidery on their wings would fly and frolic.

However, he did not sleep that night. He was not even listening to what his parents were saying. He sat thinking, looking at the mountain ranges afar. There were no lights on the mountaintop. His mother noticed that his face, which was generally pleasant, was gloomy.

'What happened to you?'

'Nothing,' he shook his head.

'Must have quarrelled with your friends,' she said.

'No.'

'Didn't have lunch?'

'Yes.'

'Then?'

'Then, nothing.'

'There is something,' she was sure. 'It is so unlike you.'

'Nothing … but…'

'But … tell us whatever it is,' his father intervened.

Then he narrated the story of the tyre that burst.

'A pity.' His mother said to his father. 'It is all due to you. I'll always say that. What he needs is hard blows with a cane … And how will it be possible? You don't even threaten him with a cane. Children don't bother about mother's caning. If you have only one, use the pestle to strike, is the saying.'

'But do you even have a pestle here?'

'If you don't have, get one made.' She was mad with rage.

'Then what happened?'

'They got the tyre changed and left.'

'Where to?'

'Downwards. Probably to the hospital.'

'So sad. Whoever taught you to be so naughty?' She turned to him with renewed anger.

'No, don't do anything to him,' the father stopped her. 'He won't repeat it. Will you do anything like this again?'

He started crying in reply.

'Let it pass,' his father said. 'After all you didn't want any of it to happen, no?'

The next day, towards morning, he noticed someone sitting by his bed. He had not slept even at that time.

'You didn't sleep?' It was his father.

'Let it go.' He repeated. 'It was not intentional.'

'It was intentional.' He was still sobbing. 'We placed the broken glass for bursting the tyre.'

'Why burst the tyres?'

'The vehicles were not stopping despite blowing the whistle. So …'

'The common whistle will not do for that. There is another kind of whistle. We will get one,' his father said, thinking about something else.

'I don't want it anymore,' the child said, amidst sobs.

'Mmm. It is alright. Don't cry. Such things happen when you are a child.'

'What would have happened to her?' he asked with hesitation.

'Who?'

'The woman who was taken to the hospital.'

'She would have been taken to the hospital. And they would have given her medicines.'

'But…'

'That is how it is. You go to sleep.'

'*Achcha* (father), will you go and find out?'

'What?'

'What happened to that grandma…'

'What will happen?' He smiled. 'I have my work to attend to, no?'

'When you get time in between…'

He was thinking about the massive engines in his workplace. Their revolving wheels, the iron bars joining them. An unending roar boomed in his ears.

'Shall I also come?'

He looked keenly at his son's face. He was reminded of his father, seeing those grief-stricken eyes. He then recalled another boy who used to wait for his father, who was a woodcutter.

'You sleep now. Let it be morning and then we will think about it.' He caressed his son's forehead with his coarse palm.

But the child did not sleep. His mind was in pain, as if pierced by a sharp glass piece.

~

The next day the boy's father took him along on his way to work. He wanted to buy a set of clothes for the child on the way back, he had told his wife. Had to get it stitched before the school re-opened. Better to buy the cloth early before the shops get crowded.

'It is me who buy all his clothes, isn't it?' the mother asked, 'Why this now?'

'He has grown up. We'll buy from a better shop,' the father said.

But he did not go to his factory or to the textile shop. He went to hospitals with the child.

It was rush time in the first hospital. They had to stand in queue at the information counter.

'Tell me the name of the patient. How can I locate someone without a name?' The girl at the counter asked them.

'We do not know her name,' said the boy.

'She is an old woman,' his father tried to help.

'Oh … How many old people come here every day, do you know?'

'An equally old man was there along with her,' his father chipped in.

'There is no point in such things, brother. Please stand aside. Next!'

It was more or less the same story in the next hospital too. How could anyone help them with so little information? It was noon by the time they made a round of three hospitals. They went to a restaurant.

'You say he went to the hospital driving the car, you are sure?' the father asked him during lunch. He said he was sure the car went down the hill. He had spotted the car negotiating turnings and curves.

'Perhaps he went down the road to a certain distance and then turned back and returned home. He may have planned to come back today morning,' father said.

They had their food ruminating over various possibilities.

'There is no need to come to such hospitals merely for breathlessness. The juice of certain herbal plants is good enough,' father said. '*Adalodakam.* Only that it will be quite bitter,' he added.

After finishing lunch they went to another hospital.

'This is the last,' father said. 'There are no more hospitals here, within my knowledge. If we don't find them here also, it means that they haven't got admitted. We will have to return.'

It was a small hospital. No rush at all. The lady at the information counter was in a post-lunch siesta.

'Oh, that is right. Last night, no? An old man had come here,' she recollected. 'We also helped to get her out. Doctor was not there at that time.'

'And then?'

'Oh, there was actually no point in a doctor. She was so cold … I knew she was dead the moment I touched her. But who am I to say that? Let the doctor come and announce it,' I thought.

'She died?' father asked.

'Yes. Why doubt? It was quite late by the time the doctor arrived and the papers were ready. She was taken away today morning. In the same car. Fortunately a driver came here just in time. But, who was she to you?'

'Just someone I know by sight,' father said.

'Poor woman…' the lady at the counter commented (without any grief).

'And then where was she taken to?' the child asked his father.

'Must have been to her home,' he said. He then asked the woman, 'Can you tell us where she lived?'

She opened a fat register, with an absolute lack of enthusiasm and slowly started turning its pages, one by one.

~

Next Sunday, the father got into a bus going to the top of the mountain, along with his son. It was for the first time he was going to the mountaintop. All these years he used to watch the travellers going up with craving. Now for the first time he too was ascending the mountain, like them. He watched the landscape rolling by. Light filtered through the branches of tall trees. Steep rocks could be seen on looking down, as also the curving route the bus had covered. There were vehicles that looked like toys plying on them. The bus travelled through the loneliness of the forest.

~

By noon the bus stopped at a very small market with a sprinkling of small shops. Father and son got down and went to the teashop right in front and enquired about the address.

The shopkeeper pointed further up and said, 'See, there it is. You have to walk some distance. Or if you wait, there is an auto rickshaw expected.'

'We'll walk,' the child said.

'What is there to eat?' Father asked.

'I don't serve meals here. The morning's batter for dosa is still there. I can give you dosa. Only that it will be slightly sour.'

The day was bright, but the sunlight was cold. The child was freezing. After climbing up for some distance, they entered a large grassland. A few cows were grazing on the ground. A huge tree stood at one end of the ground. A village lane went down from beyond the tree. The shopkeeper had directed them up to this point. 'Once you reach there, then there is nothing to worry. That lane will take you to the house. It is easy to locate the house, because there is only one house in that area,' he had said.

They walked through the lane for a few minutes and then could see an old house standing alone. There were overgrown trees and bushes all around the house. The boundary of the house was marked by bushes. The iron gates, which had two lions as sentinels, were wide open. The gates were either never closed or it has never been closed ever since it was built. Creepers had climbed up the iron sheets of the gate. The soiled walls of the house could be seen behind it. The house looked more like an abandoned inn.

This may not be the house. There are no signs of any one living here.

Then the kid saw the old car with faded paint parked in the courtyard. 'This is the house.' He was sure.

~

There was no one in the courtyard.

But then the boy saw him on an easy chair near the veranda. He didn't seem to have noticed them. Slightly open mouth, spectacles on the nose, an open book on his chest…

'He is sleeping,' said the boy.

He woke up on hearing that. He removed his spectacles and looked at them.

'Hey no, I was not sleeping. Just a nap,' It was quite obvious that he had no idea who they were. 'Who are you?'

They did not respond.

'Come, sit down. Where are you from?'

The father pointed to the valley. 'We are coming from there.'

'What is the matter?'

'We came to meet you. He wanted it.'

The old man looked at the boy. Oh, such children are rare in these times. He was quite surprised.

He took the book off his chest and placed it on the veranda.

'Have you had your lunch? It is past noon.'

'Yes,' they replied in unison.

'If you haven't, we'll have to prepare something. Because there is nothing to eat here. I don't usually have any lunch. I have a late breakfast and then something or the other for supper. The driver fetches it for me…'

'There is no one with you?'

'Yes, there was. She was the one who passed away.'

The father and son looked at each other. Neither of them spoke.

'Shall I make coffee?' The old man asked. 'It is easy.'

'We had coffee,' the father said.

'Doesn't matter. You can have one more.' He stood up.

How tall he is! The kid looked at him with awe. However he was quite old. As if he has become older since he last saw him. 'How come men become this old?', he started thinking.

~

They watched him prepare coffee with utmost care, taking out sugar, milk powder and coffee powder from thick glass jars. He did not let them join him. 'It is so easy; it will take only a minute,' he kept on saying intermittently, as if he were strengthening his case. His movements were very sluggish. The smell of kerosene spread everywhere, from the old stove.

The child was observing everything very keenly. All jars and containers had labels such as 'sugar', 'coffee' and 'milk powder' on them. He was wondering why it was necessary.

Pouring coffee into glasses, the old man said, 'All these jars are very old. Very old jars. Acquired when we were in Jalandhar. You get good jars and plates there. When we were living in the valley, we labeled all containers. So that we don't get mixed up. I was the one who did it. My wife asked me to do it. It was a good thing that we did it. Anyone can get what they want without hassles.'

'Do you know, there is a trick to fool the ants?' The old man turned to the kid as if revealing a great secret. 'Label this sugar jar with tea or coffee and ants will no more come near it.' He laughed loudly. 'Most of the ants know Malayalam. It won't do in Jalandhar. The ants there do not know Malayalam.'

The kid was enjoying the old man's talk. But something was nagging him and he did not even smile.

'Listen mate,' the old man called his father. 'Are you aware how good a kid your son is? You cannot find such children these days. He had the goodwill to help an old man. That was the surprise. I really appreciate that. You can be proud of him.'

The father looked at the child. He averted his glance.

'You take my case. My children are not like him. Of course, it is true that they are all grown up. They do not have adequate time even for their own affairs. I had never devoted my time for them when they were kids. My problem was that I continued to be a soldier in my personal life also. Everything had to be exact … And that was how it was, with school and drill and studies. They continued the same pattern when they became adults. They came when their mother departed and the very next day they were off with their bag and baggage.'

'So that was what I was coming to. Your son came to me when I was stranded on the road and he asked me in what way he could help me. I knew that he was just a child. He couldn't be of much help to me. But he came. He was with me for the rest of the day.'

They were sipping the coffee. The father felt that all was not okay with the coffee: it could have been the milk powder or was it the coffee powder gone stale…?

~

'Still, going to the hospital, finding out details and coming in search of me … I don't understand. And a young man like you traversing all this distance based on your son's words … Maybe it is a problem of my memory. Have we met before this…?'

'Now, that is…'

'Tell me, is there anything you want me to do for you?'

'No … It's none of that sir.'

The old man looked at him keenly, sipping his coffee.

'Look sir, I don't know how to present it to you. But none of it was intentional,' the father said, finishing his coffee.

Though he could not understand what the father was trying to say, the old man nodded slowly.

'I too was very naughty in my childhood. I wouldn't concentrate on my studies. I would quarrel with other kids, would trouble my teachers in every way possible, pelt stones at mango trees … and I used to be thrashed like anything by my father. With his bare hands, with the three fingers that were left on his right hand. My father was a wood cutter. Two of his fingers were shorn off by the saw. But the marks it would leave … It was always very painful. I used to hope that those three fingers would also be cut off. My father died. Yes, while sawing only. I get upset when I think of those things. Now he acting like this … He has made a mistake, a big mistake. But nothing was intentional. You see, kids do not understand the seriousness of things.'

'I don't understand what you are saying. Where do you work? My wretched memory! We've not even introduced ourselves.'

'I am a mechanic in one of the factories in the valley,' the father said.

They spoke about the house on the hill slope and the making of that house.

'I was a soldier,' the old man said. 'I retired as a major. Have you seen soldiers?' he asked the boy.

He had not seen soldiers.

'I'll show you the uniform of a major. Each rank has different badges. The lines on jackets will vary. Their numbers will also differ. There is difference even in the cap.'

The old man talked about the places he had lived in while in service. He seemed to be like a loner who was eager to talk about all this to someone.

'I have a flat in the town just about a kilometre from your factory. It is locked up now. I lived there for many years. After I left the army…'

'When did you retire?'

The old man tried to recollect. When was it? When was it? Just as the lustre of medals dim through years, memories too become dim.

He could however remember the darkness in the corridor leading to their apartment. It was not really darkness, but the shadow of the huge building nearby. Despite thinking in details about the period he had lived in that apartment, he could not correctly determine his living there. He felt that another massive shadow had spread over his memories.

'Well, it has been quite sometime since I retired,' he said at last. 'Certainly after the war. In nineteen ….' creases appeared on his forehead.

'I have participated in three wars,' he said as if for a compromise. 'Three wars…'

~

'What kids sometime do could be unpardonable misdeeds,' said the father of the boy. 'Only that we did not understand it when we were kids. But, but none of this was intentional.'

'Intentional, yes, sometimes it can happen that way too,' the old man said.

'It just happened so. However, since it happened and since I sensed that he felt bad, I also felt like meeting you.'

The old man had not yet understood what was it all about. He again tried to decipher whether he had any sort of contact with this man. No, what he is trying to say is something totally different. He thought that there is a huge shadow spread across memories too.

'Kids…' when the father tried to speak again, the old man stopped him.

'You are speaking again about children. Why children? I just don't understand what you are trying to say. Which kids? Perhaps you are speaking to the wrong person?'

'We came to meet you only.'

'Okay. You already said that. And I know this kid. But I just don't understand why you are speaking about kids and the blunders they commit. I don't recall having ever seen you.'

The child's father spoke about the houses on the hill slope. Kids who are on their own in these houses. Their sharpened glass mischief … Gradually, that evening and his journey that got disrupted half-way reappeared in words. By the time he completed the narration, the kid's eyes were brimming over.

'Let's go out for some time,' the old man said. Cows have been let out for grazing. That boy sometimes will take a nap sitting somewhere. He is not going to know if some of them overstep at the slope and fall down.

'We had seen the cows when we came,' the kid's father said.

'This was a lucky break. This grassland. The ground is full of grass all the time,' the old man said walking in the front.

'Sir, you brought up all these cows?' Father asked.

'That boy is there for all that. I just go along with him, that's all. I got these cows along with the house. When the previous owner left this place, he handed them over to me. I thought it would be a good idea to become familiar with someone.'

They walked through the open iron gates. The sun was shining, but the same cold sunlight. The kid walked just behind the old man. After going some distance, the old man turned and looked at him. There was neither anger nor hatred in those eyes, the kid noticed.

'Do not play with glass,' he said. 'Sometimes your own fingers would get cut. Won't it become a disaster if it happens when no one is there in the house?'

'He won't do it again,' father said from behind.

The old man laughed silently.

'Look, you don't have to get upset. There would not have been any change in my wife's condition, even if you had not placed the glass and the tyre had not burst. I'm not speaking about a human being's span of life, etc., but that was the reality. No change was possible, I know.' He stopped for a moment and said slowly, 'because she was dead before I started with her from here.'

The shocked child stared at him. The image of the woman who was lying motionless on the back seat of the slightly tilted car slowly spread in his mind.

By that time they had reached the ground. The cows were relaxing under the trees at the end of the grassland.

~

'You must be wondering why I drove all this distance, if I knew it all,' he asked.

'It was due to my guilty conscience,' the old man said slowly. 'Guilty conscience … the feeling that I had done something grievously wrong … taking out the car after so many years, driving through the mountain passes with great strain … that was the only reason. Hasn't such a little boy come searching for me? What for? If you hadn't come I would never have even suspected such a thing. How natural it is for a car tyre to burst! But this baby, the pain he underwent. That was how it was for me too.'

'And moreover, why should someone who has been bedridden for years be taken to hospital when death comes? Does anyone have any suspicions about the death? "Was she still alive?" was the question others had when they heard about the death. A death that was taken for granted by even her children and close relatives. In retrospect, it was a totally unwarranted journey. And the sleepless night spent in the hospital.'

'But at the same time, not even one moment in life, not any kind of journey is unwarranted, one feels sometime. While coming down the mountain and while keeping vigil for the dead body of one with whom I had cohabitated for years, I was thinking about my life and nothing else. Many images have faded away, but several, at least a few, will always remain in our memory till death. My mind was full of such images.'

'I was a soldier, I had told you. No, an excellent soldier who participated in three wars and one who led from the front. How many medals I got for meritorious service! And what acclaims! It was a great time. At last, when my service was over, after our children had reached top positions, we settled down in a place that was familiar to us. I had told you that I too lived in the town where you work. In a flat … two beings who loved each other, a couple who understood each other. We were models for neighbours and friends. Young people would approach us for guidance, blessings.'

'But there was a huge building near our flat. The massive shadow of the building would envelope our corridor. Light in the corridor was always reluctant to show itself. Or was it darkness … who knows!'

They could see the shadow of the tree under which the cows had huddled, lengthening in the distance. The boy taking care of the grazing cattle, gazed at the top of the hills and hooted.

'Isn't it like the fading of light?' the old man asked no one in particular. 'Minute variations started appearing in her behaviour. Something like forgetfulness. Inability to recall where certain things were kept. Or unable to recognise things in daily use … Then we started labelling the containers. Coffee, sugar, etc., good enough for even ants to understand! But after some time, even that could be of no help. Because, what is sugar? Or what is to be made out of milk powder? Unable to remember the utility of things … each room getting closed one by one. Even alphabets vanishing into oblivion…'

~

'However, something else too happened. Certain memories got sharper. That was the surprise. Very old incidents … the journeys we went on during the early days of our wedding … tidbits of jokes and fun. How we used to scold children when they were very little, the anxieties of war … our youngest son going missing during an excursion, and locating him soaked to the skin and shivering at a shop veranda….'

'As time passed she became irritable and began to get angry for minor things. She would scold for little slip-ups. I dismissed them with a smile; as it is we were used to little skirmishes between us. But this was not the same. I began to feel that there is a place for hatred too between two human beings, just like love. She recalled certain incidents, which had occurred long back and had been forgotten. And arguing about it as if all that happened only the previous day. Some of my shortcomings, my blunders, which I never knew that she knew. It affected me badly that she was aware of it all these years. The perception that she was concealing all that from me as a concession or favour done to me was devastating. The shock that love was just a cocoon, and that we were just cohabiting under a shadow. Many things which we do not even utter for decency's sake, returned in the surge of memories and I was swept away by the waves.'

'In those days, it happened only once in a while. We behaved normally when we returned to reality. That there are layers in the relation between human beings, that beyond the smiles and words, which we wear like shirts, the knowledge that the smell and boredom of the body remains when the dress is shorn off … even when we act as if everything is normal, the hatred and indignation remains undigested somewhere inside … two massive isolations that lived together for half a century and tolerated each other. Do you understand me? We never trusted one another after that. That was the truth.'

'The chasm between us enlarged as time passed. She hated seeing me, I felt my profession, my pride in having been a soldier, all that peeled off me. She had no hesitation in scolding me loudly. Gradually others began to notice it. The attitude of people towards us changed. Our neighbours looked at us as two quarrelsome human beings with nothing to unite us. There being nothing that can be concealed in a human life … secrets having no value … think of such a state of affairs. How can a human being be a human being without a nook or corner that is not open to others? How can I explain all that to you?'

'I decided to leave that place without waiting for long. Somewhere far off, where no one would see us, where we will not have any contact with anyone we know. It was that search that brought me here to this mountain.'

~

'Our first days here … it was a big relief in the beginning. True, it is not like the life in town; there are many limitations. Having lived a soldier's life, I could accept any living conditions with a favourable attitude. However, it did not have any effect on our relationship. My wife continued to scold and curse me as was her wont. That there was no one to hear it, was the only consolation.'

'Luckily—I don't know what you might think when I put it that way—luckily she had many ailments. That helped her to stay indoors most of the time. The winter in the mountains laid her up. She was troubled by wheezing. She lay there with her eyes staring and chest raised, struggling for breath, as if not even the smallest quantity of air is available anywhere in this earth. And each breath she took was accompanied by a large sound.'

'In spite of all this, her curse words came in search of me in the interval of inhaling and exhaling. There was no change in that. Not only that, things were in such a state that one would wonder whether such words would emerge from the mouth of a grand educated lady. "Wretched creature, bloody…." So many words, abusive words that cannot be uttered, forgive me; I cannot go into details since this child is here. I ignored them all. She was not targeting me, I feigned. I consoled myself saying, "She is sick". I gave her medicines and food with absolute regularity.'

'Thus, it became a habit I should say. But the thought that I've become all alone started nagging me. I was reduced to the desolation of this forest. I tried to befriend the animals and birds. I became well-versed in their routines. Then I understood how simple this world is. We have been trying to make it into a serious affair with laws and drills and parades.'

'But yet, a human being attaches high value to his selfish needs and silly privacies. Knowing that there is nothing in it. In such weak moments, his controls fail and he falls down into trifles.'

~

'That was one such day for me. Maybe because I was late going to bed or maybe because I couldn't sleep for quite a long time, I was late getting up in the morning. It was already quite bright when

when I was up. Must have been eight at least. "Oh, so late," I thought. I could hear my wife's loud breathing from her bedroom.

'When I went into her room there was an overpowering stench. It was the smell of excreta. Usually a bed pan is used and she would call. Today I was late. I couldn't even stand in the room.'

'"Where were you?" She asked. I didn't answer.'

'"Gone to war?" she asked with derision.'

'I was thinking about how to change the sheet and clean her body.'

'I went out and returned with a big bucket of water. I made up a cleaning solution, sprayed Dettol. I got her to get up from the bed and made her sit, leaning on to the wall. I could see her bedsores worsening.'

'All the while she was sitting silent looking intently at me. I had noticed a wild sort of revenge in her eyes. I evaded her staring eyes and tried to concentrate on work.'

'"This is the work that suits you," she said. "You are fit for only this." I made a bundle of the bedspread and the blanket soiled by sweat and excreta and threw it out of the room.'

'"You are fit only for this." I could hear her saying this feebly. "What is the point in your being anything else! There is no point in saying that you were a Major in the army, you had fought in wars."'

'I could hear the sounds of cows being taken out of the shed. The boy has come. He will them give water and also feed them. Then he will take them for grazing.'

'"And what war, after all? It is for the poor soldiers to stand in the front and be shot! The likes of you will eat and drink and enjoy and flaunt about as big bosses."'

'I tried to clean up the dirt underneath the cot with a grass broom.'

'"You thought no one would know? Military boss! You have kept them inside no, those old coats and uniforms. And also those useless medals! Throw it away. At least that space will become clean." She raised her voice.'

'I'm cleaning, can't you see?'

'"Oh, this!" She laughed. She went on laughing and now she had difficulty in breathing.'

'"My sweeper! Why do you need those medals! In what way are you eligible for those medals?" She laughed again.'

'"Keep quiet," I looked at her and ordered in a strict voice.'

'She didn't seem to have expected it. She didn't speak but stared at me with increased violence. Breathlessness again caught up with her and she started coughing. I just stood still looking at her, not knowing why she was coughing in that manner. I did not attempt to go to her and massage her back or fan her.'

'She stopped coughing after a long bout. I knew her mouth was full of phlegm. Somehow, I felt sorry for her. I walked towards the window sill to take the cup from there and to ask her to spit the phlegm into it.'

'Then she spat the entire phlegm in her mouth on to my face.'

~

'It was not anger, but insult was my sentiment then. I felt I was going down. Like a slave who could be transacted, I had become a creature that can barely breathe for existence, with neither expectations nor hopes. I wiped the filth from my body and cleaned the floor. I spread fresh linen on the bed. I lifted that body and laid it down on the bed and went back to the kitchen without uttering a single word.'

'I kept asking myself, "What is happening to me?" So many soldiers have stood motionless in front of me waiting for my orders and I have meted out punishment to so many. I have altered the course of life of so many with just one decision. But now, here in the midst of this forest, helpless, unable to take any decision, getting used to immense loneliness, continuing like this, subservient to rebukes and curses. What is the meaning of all this? Is it an imprisonment? If so, is it a lifelong sentence? Which fate has sentenced me like this without even a trial?'

'I didn't go to her to give her food or medicine. I remained there with my own thoughts. She is a diabetic, and hence lack of food can cause problems. But I didn't go that side. And I too did not eat anything. I was not hungry. I continued in a state where all hunger is extinguished.'

'I heard a call from my wife's room at about noon. I did not bother. It was repeated after sometime. This time it was louder. I could make out 'water'. She must be thirsty. Still, I didn't feel like going to her. I slowly rubbed my face which had been stained by phlegm. I recalled all the abuses and insulting words I was subjected to during all these years. I sat there unmoving, unable to move, like an old donkey bearing soiled clothes, much more than one could carry on one's back in a lifetime.'

'The sound from the other room became feeble. Then it became quite weak. A mysterious joy had seized me. Every time she called, I experienced the liberation of a slave. I lay down on my easy chair. A small walkway in front, beyond that the iron gates wide open. It was covered by grass and creepers. Nobody there. Nothing. Only the wild growl of solitude. I was too tired and fell into a short sleep.'

'I was brought back to reality by the surroundings. What was happening? A sick woman speaking or doing something out of the way, due to her unsound mind and I react so cruelly! My body started shivering. Am I a human being? Doesn't the lesson of war teach that even the enemy who is helpless should be regarded with respect? How did I go wrong? Why did I forget all that so easily? I rushed to the room.'

'Those eyes were open. I saw helplessness spread over those eyes in which the flame of revenge was blazing all through these days. I fancied that this is not the reality and that when I touch her she will get up and curse me with the same rage she always displayed.'

'Slowly I raised the body from which all the weight of life had oozed out. I was melting in the fire of great sin. All that I wanted from her then was a rebuke, or even a punishment. The expectation arose in me that I will be able to infuse breath into her body by sprinkling some magic water. I decided to take my vehicle out after a very long time.'

~

They were still standing in the grassland. The ground seemed to be a green sea in the evening sun. Grass stirred like waves in the light breeze. The old man gazed into the distance. Cows walked into the range of his vision and the boy with a long stick behind them. The red sun was ready to sink beyond the hills. Snow-white clouds.

The bus slowly started the descent. It was quite cold. They could hear the noises of the birds come to roost on the tall trees. It was twilight.

The bus travelled further down. When it reached a plain below the mountains, they could see the three houses along the slopes, lost in deep thought, like three wise men.

Lamps in the houses were lit. There were also the same three pale stars in the sky behind the houses, lighting the way.

Three Blind Men Describe an Elephant

One of our visiting faculty was Kuruvila, a journalist who was with a foreign newspaper for a couple of years. He nursed a sort of contempt for India, especially the media activities here. Kuruvila would occasionally come up with new projects, as if to prod and provoke us. A report on an altogether new issue, a scoop which had nothing obscene about it, an imaginary interview, two different editorials on the same theme … such were the projects he generally rammed on us. Whatever be our efforts in response, Kuruvila would find something or the other in them to ridicule us with. Hence, some of us were intent on a story that would floor him beyond redemption.

I was living in an old lodge that was rather cheaply priced. Among the inmates, I was the only one who was a student. All the others were either middle-aged government officials, who were eagerly waiting for a transfer to their hometown or small-time shopkeepers. The lodge consisted of two buildings facing each other, separated only by a little distance. The top floors of these buildings were connected by a wide cement bridge. Access to the top floor was provided by an old wooden staircase. One had to be very careful going up and down the staircase; the sound of the railings loosening was all too audible and nerve-wracking.

I knew that there were three blind men living in the room across mine. But I had not met them nor bothered about them. I did run into one or two of them at some nook or corner of the city on rare occasions, but that was all. It would be more correct to say that I did not see anything special in them other than their being blind.

But that Saturday, I had a hard look at them, even as I was lazing around in the room doing nothing in particular. They were going out. All three came out of the room and one of them locked the door. He bolted the door and inserted the key with precision. Then they walked in a row, crossed the cement bridge connecting the two buildings and reached the staircase. Gently tapping the wooden step, as if confirming its strength, they climbed down. The rumbling of the loose railings remained in the air for some time.

I was baffled. Three blind men living together on the second floor without any assistance from anyone else. Who were they? How did they become a threesome? Their decent attire and the fact that they were living in a lodge dispelled in me the images of mendicants, which we generally tend to associate with the blind. Maybe it was the curiosity they aroused in me that made me scan my memory for those blind men with whom I was acquainted in the past. Apart from a beggar or two, there was hardly anyone.

I walked to the end of the corridor to see where they were. They had already crossed the road and reached the other side. After a few minutes, two of them got into a bus and the third started walking in the opposite direction after confirming his position with his walking stick. I stood there till he gradually vanished from my sight. The road was not very crowded at that time of the day and there were not many people at the bus stop. And even those who were there, seemed to ignore the scene as an everyday happening.

Back in my room, I thought of Kuruvila and his boastful classroom sessions. Why not make these blind men the subject of a project? The life of three blind men—their livelihood, accommodation, food and their conversations? But could I be making myself a target of Kuruvila's ridicule? It was then that the old proverb, 'just as the blind saw the elephant' came to my mind. In fact, it is more than a proverb; it is a sort of comment on their inadequacy—that they can see the elephant only in parts and not in its entirety. This, I felt is an apt subject. What ideas of an elephant do my neighbouring blind men carry? However, they also could be aware of this proverb. If I abruptly started a discussion on this, they may feel offended. I had to be careful in introducing it.

I remained in the room indulging in absolute lethargy till about four in the evening, even skipping lunch. I came out after a bath and wandered about the city without any definite destination. There was a cricket match that day and there were crowds in front of TV showrooms. It was when I saw the threesome in such a crowd that the idea of an interview with them revived in me. But how did they get involved in this cricket-mad crowd?

I stood at a distance and watched. I remained there till they left for the nearby bus stop, talking to one another. It was past six by then.

I returned to the lodge by half past seven. Instead of heading for my room, I walked through the veranda and up to the room where they were staying. The door was closed. One could hear them talking, albeit indistinctly. I knocked gently.

'The door is not locked. Please come in,' a voice boomed from the room.

I opened the door. They were sitting on a grass-mat on the floor. They seemed to be huddled together closer to each other than people generally did. The room was well-lit. A high-power bulb was being used, presumably to overcome the low-voltage problem plaguing the city. The unnaturalness of these three, who couldn't see, sitting in bright light surprised me.

It was not just that. The orderliness of the room would charm any one. Three walking sticks leaned in a far corner, in beautiful symmetry. There was only a table and chair that could be called furniture; not even a cot. Apart from a fan, whirling with a mild hum, it was absolutely peaceful in the room. There were a couple of bags and a not-very-new harmonium on the table.

'Hello!' one of the blind men greeted me.

'You can sit there,' another pointed in the direction of the chair.

'I stay in the next room…' I introduced myself, while sitting on the chair.

'We know,' all three said in unison. 'We were aware that you were coming to our room.'

'How is that? You have not seen me before.' Even though I posed this question, I was not sure of how they would understand the essence of the usage 'seen'.

'We could make out from the sound of your footfalls, on the stairs,' one of them said.

'You are a student, no?'

So they know me.

'We were discussing today's cricket match,' he continued. 'This fellow here is cricket crazy. He had placed a bet that India would win. Fortunately we were the bookies and we waived the stakes.'

'It was that silly run-out; otherwise, you would have had to pay up.'

The other two merely smiled.

'These days, even I don't have that much of interest,' the cricket fan turned to me. His eyelids were permanently closed.

But at times they seemed to move. He continued speaking: 'I too have given up, since Gavaskar retired.'

'Why?'

'All the rest are mediocre. Who else is there to stick on at the wicket?'

A general silence prevailed for some time. Then I made a coughing sound to remind them of my presence.

'I clearly remember the day Gavaskar completed 10,000 runs. It was a late cut for two runs.'

'O, what a great memory!' one of them made fun of him.

'Earlier, there used to be ball-by-ball running commentary. But no one cares for it these days, with the advent of TV,' lamented the cricket fan.

'We ought to buy a TV,' said the third blind man, who had remained silent till now.

'What for? Should we usher in that mad game into this room too?' He turned to me with a smile, 'Sorry. He is a gone case. Won't stop once he starts talking cricket.'

'It's alright. I walked in only to meet you.'

'That's indeed nice of you.' The cricket fan extended his hand to me and said, 'My name is Sekhar. I'm a telephone operator.' Shaking my hand, he mentioned the name of the institution he was working for.

It struck me that I was holding the hand of a blind man for the first time in my life.

'I'm a music teacher,' said the next one. 'I give music tuitions at a few houses.'

'What's your name?

'Reghuraman. This harmonium is mine.' He got up, took the harmonium, sat down on the mat and played randomly for a moment. The crystal balls in his eyes were moving.

I also introduced myself.

'My name is Chandran,' the third one said. 'I don't have a big job. I'm not much educated too.' There seemed to be a tinge of disappointment in his tone. 'I'm a tourist guide now.'

'Guide?' I couldn't restrain myself from asking. The astonishment in my question didn't seem to affect him.

'But not a guide who takes people all around the city.' He explained that he worked as a guide in an ancient temple, which lay just outside the city.

That temple is famous for its marvellous sculptures. He, who can't see them for himself, shows them to the visitors.

Hoping that a measure of intimacy had been established between us, I was emboldened to broach the subject, but with great humility and deliberately making it sound a matter of vital importance. I was still apprehensive whether they would explode at me.

However, all three of them took it with due seriousness. Even though so worn out as to be a cliché, they were not affected by the narrowness of the proverb of the blind seeing an elephant. It was also possible that beyond such accusations, they may have been contemplating the quintessence of the proverb.

Sekhar reminisced, abandoning the pleasant demeanour he had, while discussing cricket.

'It was a long time ago, when I was a child. Ours was a large family. Many others relatives and friends, would throng the house during the week-long festival at the village temple. They would keep on going to the temple and back, irrespective of whether it was day or night.'

'As far as I was concerned, a recollection of the festival was always redolent of sweet and succulent Arabian dates. No one would take me to the festival site. Even if someone chaperoned me, they would let me listen to the percussion band from a distance and then lead me home. But, one day, one of the grown-up boys took me to the festival ground. He was a cousin who studied in a distant town.

'All the way to the temple, we were accosted by people returning from the fair. Some were laughing loudly and some, they maybe children, crying out and blowing horns. Ice-cream vendors with their typical horns added to the melee. The crowd and the rush increased as we approached the festival ground. I was firmly holding on to the hands of my companion.'

'Thus, for the first time, I heard the percussion instruments at close quarters. The drums rolled in a tremendous high pitched climax, like the growling of mad bees. The crowd was jam-packed, jostling each other. One could breathe in the smell of the sweat of the others around.

'Suddenly…' Sekharan's facial muscles became taut. Some kind of terror seemed to overpower him. His white eyeballs wobbled. A strange loneliness seemed to seize him, as if there were no one else in the room.

'Suddenly friends, my surroundings, which till then seemed to be firm and immobile, started to move. And it was happening too fast. The closely packed crowd, which had seemed like a rock wall till then, dispersed in a moment. Someone shouted that the elephant had run amok. I fell down in the stampede. Some jumped over me, while some trampled me. I had lost hold of my cousin's hand. I tried to get up. But every time more people stumbled over me and I repeatedly fell down. My whole body was burning. After some time, I experienced a silence and vacancy all around me as if there were nobody left in the festival ground. I slowly raised myself and sat down. I couldn't do anything beyond that. I started crying, not knowing in which direction to move.'

It was as if we too had been transplanted into his helplessness. Maybe we had forgotten that he was the only one stranded alone.

'Then came an earthshaking sound. It was coming closer. Not at a quick pace. But each footstep had a terrifying resonance. Friends, please believe me. That sound passed quite close to me, (or was it over me…?).' Then he tried to simulate that movement as loud as possible. The closed eyelids trembled in the force he exerted.

Sekharan remained silent for a few minutes. Everyone seemed to be caught in a web of terror.

'I've never gone to festivals thereafter. When this friend here referred to the elephant, I heard that rumbling sound. For me, the elephant is that gigantic movement, pal. It is a series of episodes. None of them have an existence of its own, in isolation. The percussion instruments that suddenly fell silent, my fall, people running helter-skelter, those noises floating above the eerie silence … the whirl of the world, that passed me by as I lay forlorn.'

Sekharan did not speak after that. Was he recollecting the whole incident once again?

'Mine is not a singular experience, as that of Sekharan,' Reghuraman, the music teacher broke the silence that was prevailing in the room. "I experience it frequently.'

'What does that mean?' I asked.

'I frequently dream of elephants.'

'Dreaming?'

'Yes, once or twice, even a herd of elephants.'

'How do you see dreams?' My curiosity increased. Let alone an elephant, how can a blind man have dreams! Suddenly I was afraid whether my question had upset him.

'I can't explain certain things,' he turned to me and continued. 'But what I said is true. I have certainly seen a herd of elephants in a dream. But they have not terrified me like Sekharan's narration.'

'How do you see?' I asked. He looked at me as if he did not comprehend my question.

'Without light … how can you see without light?'

'Why should there be light in a dream?' Reghuraman asked after a short pause, 'or, what is light?'

'Light … what I mean is…' Instead of spelling it out in words, I thought of pointing to the burning bulb in the room, but gave it up realising the futility of it.

Then I said slowly, 'There is light in this room.'

'Yes, yes...' one of the other two mumbled.

'That's why one sees,' I explained.

But, what is sight? The curiosity on his countenance baffled me.

'But still you see dreams?' I asked.

'I'm certain about it. But you won't understand that.'

'Elephants have never appeared in my dreams,' I felt I was standing still, at the very same point where I'd begun.

'But you have seen elephants, no? Please don't misunderstand me,' he said bending low in humility. 'What was the elephant you saw like?'

The interview was leading to a crisis, I felt. How could I describe an elephant to this poor man? I became aware of my language losing its lustre and also obtaining a dark pallor. I was as helpless as a carpenter who has many tools but doesn't know how to use them.

The blind men were waiting with keen attention to hear me speak.

'You know that the colour of the elephant is black? Only its tusks are white.' I continued, desperately searching for an object with similarity, familiar to them. 'Like a bus, as huge as a bus.'

'Is the elephant like a bus?' Reghuraman asked.

'Not exactly, but in size…'

'Elephant is a whirl, a tumble,' Sekharan ruminated. 'Reghu, haven't you heard a bus growling?'

'Okay, pal,' Reghuraman said, as if extending an affectionate invitation. 'If you could enter the space where I have my dreams, you would also see the herd of elephants,' he continued laughing loudly. 'This is all I can say. As it is, I'm not good at storytelling.'

I merely smiled, rather naively.

'Ganapathy is my favourite god,' Reghuraman announced. Then he started playing the harmonium and sang a composition of Dikshitar in praise of Lord Ganesha.

'I too love elephants,' Chandran, the guide said, shuffling his glasses. 'I know all the elephant sculptures in the temple, with all their details and nuances. Some of the elephants in the front row do not have tusks and some have broken tusks.'

'May be Ganapathy,' Chandran tried to guess.

'No, the tusks were broken during an invasion in the past. Now the government takes care of them,' He said, correcting us.

'I have this craze for elephants from childhood. No, it was not developed from going for festivals. Somehow elephants were always around. The ones brought to the river for giving them a bath ... mahouts coming to our house demanding palm-leaves for feeding them ... I had a ring made of the hair from the elephant's tail. The trumpeting of elephants still reverberates in my mind and I also remember the commands given to the elephants for moving about. I've even touched an elephant once.'

'Really!' Sekharan, who had experienced an elephant through earth-shaking tremors, was stupefied.

'But I was not thrilled. I knew that this was not my elephant. I wanted an elephant that I could hold in my fists, touch all over and know.'

'Like the stone elephants,' I mumbled.

'Not even that, another which would always be mine,' he paused for a moment. 'Everyone in my village, used to get themselves tattooed. It was done on the skin with a needle. They were pictures etched with the help of a chemical. It would leave an impression in, they say, green. It will never fade away, a figure on the skin. Most of them were pictures of gods and goddesses; Hanuman, Vishnu, Devi…'

He took off his dark glasses. Pale in colour, the eyelids had a kind of nakedness around them.

'I have seen tattoos of conch shells,' I said.

'Yes, they do all such figures. But I wanted only an elephant. But the tattoo-artist would not hear of it. "Will not gods suffice?" he asked. "It is going to be an elephant and if not, nothing," I told him. I wanted one that would always remain with me. I was firm.' Chandran said with pride. 'He finally agreed.'

'Where is it?' all three of us asked in unison.

Chandran hesitated for a moment. Then he shyly rolled up his lungi and exposed his hairless thigh just above the knee.

I was shocked by the distorted figure on the fair skin. That figure, which could be taken for an elephant, was standing there seamlessly, absolutely unaware of its shape. A mark which could be imagined to be the trunk, stood out like an erect phallus. A fierce trumpeting pierced my ears.

Chandran softly touched the tattoo. The other two hesitated for a few moments as if afraid of my presence. Then they too spread their fingers on the green lines and knew the elephant. I thought that Chandran was feeling awfully tickled when those fingers touched the tattoo. And also that the dimensionless, seamless elephant was throwing a challenge at me.

He rolled down the lungi and smiled mysteriously, but content. Then he put on his dark glasses and glanced at me without any emotion.

Everyone was silent for quite some time.

The old clock chimed once. It was half past nine.

I stood up and thanked them. The three blind men accompanied me to the door. As I stepped out of the room, I heard Sekharan say, 'The clock said half past nine? It is fast by at least five minutes. Friend, go fast, the power goes off at half past nine.'

I did not hurry. As soon as I opened the door of my room, the power went off, drowning everything around in pitch darkness.

I wondered if an elephant, carrying an idol of darkness, was waiting for me in the room.

Light Years

'James, I've been here before. Here, I've stood here holding on to these railings,' Kamala exclaimed, holding tightly on to the railings of the hanging bridge, listening to the gurgling sound of flowing water.

'You had mentioned this when we started,' James smiled.

'Oh, did I? But see, it was exactly here, this very spot. Just one touch and everything came back to me. That is the wonder.'

'Really?'

'Yes, James. But there was more water at that time. One could hear its sound from afar. We had come immediately after the monsoon. In those days, we were in Bangalore, you know. Why, don't you believe what I'm saying?'

'Oh, it is not a question of my believing or not, Kamala. You came here at least five years ago, right? Then how can you be so sure that you were standing at this exact spot?'

'I can James. I can see certain things you can't see, even if your eyes are wide open.'

'You always talk about eyes,' said James.

Kamala laughed aloud. 'If anything, I should at least talk about eyes, no James?'

She then became silent and just stood there trying to catch the sound of the water current.

A tourist passed by them. The railings of the hanging bridge screeched.

'Yes, I was standing like this here,' Kamala tried to recollect. It was season time and very crowded. People passed jostling and brushing against us. And the bridge was swaying vigorously. Caught up in the surge of the crowd, I almost went down. I know it was exactly at this spot. Luckily, Nandan caught hold of me. That was how he was … would always be with me, Nandan. He would always take care of me.'

'Are you upset by what I said?' James asked, zooming his camera on to the feeble water flow.

'Hey, what was there to be upset?'

'Nothing. But I spoke to you about your eyes.'

'You did not speak about my eyes. That is my complaint. Why should the eyes be blamed just because they have no vision, James? Shall I tell you something? Nandan adored my eyes. I have big eyes, he used to say. He had even lined my eyelids with kohl once.'

'Is it?'

'Yes.'

'Oh, then he must have been a mushy romantic.'

'What is this, my dear James? Is there anything wrong in lining the eyes of someone you love?'

'Who knows? But don't ever expect me to do it, Kamala.'

'James, please don't compare. Each one is different, no?'

It was quite warm, even though they were so close to the waterfall.

The fading four o' clock sun sketched shadow pictures of leaves on the sand.

They got cucumbers from wayside vendors. The cucumbers were quite cool. After taking a bite, Kamala got hers sliced and she made the vendor apply a paste of chilly powder and salt. But James felt like having a cup of tea.

'Did you take a snap of the waterfall?' Kamala asked.

'Mm,' James grunted lazily. But the camera rested on his shoulder like a dear pet.

'During outings Nandan was quite content with such simple things,' Kamala said finishing her cucumber. 'At times, one would feel that he was a spendthrift, but that was not the case. Actually it was merely due to anxiety regarding food from outside eateries, you know. "Tummy would be upset," he used to say often. But, whatever the reason, he would become thin as a stick just two days into a tour.'

James then wanted to ask her something, but he cut himself short.

Kamala laughed. 'Like a stick! How could you see it? That was the question on your tongue, no James?'

'Hey, no,' James tried to conceal his embarrassment.

'Yes dear, I know mind reading. We measure each other when we hug, isn't it James?'

'I want a cup of tea,' James said.

His cell phone buzzed, but he ignored it.

It was some distance from the waterfall to the exit through the narrow path. Exhausted, Kamala sat on a wooden bench on the side of the pavement.

It has been quite some time since I had such a long walk. 'My leg is aching,' James said. Kamala raised the edge of her sari and massaged her calf. She smelled of sweat. A few girls walked past them in the direction of the waterfall, talking loudly. Kamala with her head bent, continued massaging her calf till their voices faded out in the distance.

'Did you have a look at them?' Kamala asked.

'Whom?

'Those who went past just now, those girls.'

'No. Why?'

'You liar, you don't look at girls, eh?'

'Oh that!'

'Were they charming?'

'Maybe.'

'Why this evasion? Beauties are to be glanced at, no?'

'Oh, but how can I stare at women when I'm with you?' James smiled.

'Not women. Girls. They are young. One can make out from their talk.'

'Okay Kamala. Let it be so.'

'That was one great thing when I was with Nandan. He used to describe everything for me.'

'You must have burned with jealousy?' James asked.

'Why? I was not a child,' Kamala smiled.

'Listen to me, James. In Bangalore, we would go to one mall or the other every evening and look at the crowd of boys and girls. We would stand there discussing them. It was good fun. I shall tell you a naughty bit if you won't mock me.'

'I'm not up to mocking you. You are the master in it.'

'Thank you, James.'

'Okay. But what was it that you were about to tell me?'

'Haha, it was a joke. Where did I stop? Yes, we stand before the mall and watch the young people coming and going. Nandan would tell me that their undergarments were visible over the top of their low-waist jeans. That was the in-thing those days.'

'Then?'

'Then what? I asked Nandan to describe it to me. We had fun a whole evening taking stock of those undergarments.'

Kamala started laughing. She went on laughing till it became a bout of cough.

'You are slightly eccentric Kamala,' James said. 'Not just you, your guy too. Why he walked out on you is what I can't understand. You were actually made for each other.'

Kamala did not respond. She set right her sari and sat there idly, hands folded. Then she closed her eyes. James did not stare at the pale nudity of her eyelids. He took out his camera and tried to get a picture of a tree that had shed its leaves. Three birds were perching on the leafless branches.

His cell phone rang again. But he silenced it after a couple of rings just as before.

'Let's go,' Kamala said. 'That driver must be fed up waiting for us.'

'That is part of his job. Don't we pay him for it?'

'Why did you not take the call?' Kamala asked.

'Later on,' I thought.

'It was Elizabeth, no?'

'Yes. Why?'

'I guessed. She keeps calling you even now?'

'It is her need no; she will call again.'

'What is that big need?' Kamala asked.

'Oh that, that is nothing.'

'But still … Or will there be a problem if I am told?'

'What problem? She is the one with a problem.'

'Kamala laughed. Let me guess. A wild guess. There is something in your possession which would affect her. A letter, certain information … something of that nature. Right?'

'It is your guess, no? Why should I say whether it is right or wrong?'

'Yes that is exactly the answer to my question,' Kamala laughed. Then she became silent.

'Don't, James,' Kamala said. 'Leave her alone.'

James did not respond.

'Just leave it,' Kamala said raising her head. 'You will regret it after sometime if you do anything rash in rage. Hatred is like love; it becomes boring in course of time.'

Again James did not make any reply. He looked up and found that the birds had flown away from the branches.

'What's the name of your ex…? Oh yes, Nandan. Do you call Nandan?' He asked her all of a sudden.

'In my dreams,' Saying this, Kamala took hold of his hand. Her hands are unusually cold, he thought.

'Okay. Is this a good place,' James?

'Yeah. Why do you ask?'

'I don't know. Somehow it doesn't gel like last time.'

'Kamala, get up and stand at the edge of this bench. Yes, just like that, with your hands down … yes, now I can take a snap.'

'Right?'

'Yes. One more.'

'Why did you use flash in this daylight?'

'How do you know?'

'I know. That's all to it. Nandan never used the flash. He preferred natural light.'

When they crossed the gate and reached the parking area, the cab driver brought the vehicle to them. The taxi was arranged at the hotel in the morning. The driver was a middle-aged man. He had said that his wife was a Malayalee. Maybe because of that or out of sympathy, he was very considerate to them. It took more than an hour to reach the Buddha temple. It was twilight by then. Kamala tried to recall her visit there with Nandan.

Then they had stayed in a hotel in front of the temple, run by lamas. In the evening, they had walked along the path from the temple taking them to the interior villages. The path was secluded and deserted. Nandan did not stop walking even as darkness settled. It was a village of refugees, their homes, temple, school and small shops and then maize fields. Nandan described everything to her. On the way back, they had tea from a roadside shack. It was run by a young refugee. He had been born and brought up in that place. His motherland was only hearsay for him. Nandan was always keen about such details.

'We could have stayed in the hotel of the lamas,' said Kamala.

'That hotel may not have electricity or water, madam,' the driver said in broken Malayalam.

'But what has Kamala got to do with electricity, no?' James stopped as soon as he began.

'True,' Kamala smiled. 'Why do we always need electricity? Have not the people of yore lived without it?'

A beggar extended his hand to them, crying aloud that he was blind. James took out some change from his purse and gave it to him.

'What James, did you give him alms?'

'Poor fellow! He cannot see, no?'

'Did he become poor because he cannot see?'

'Is it not?'

'No. So I too am poor in your reckoning?'

'Never.'

'In that case, should you give alms only because he does not have eyesight?'

James did not answer. He saw in the distance the gold tinted gateway of the Buddha temple and the sun bathed in glorious light. He toyed with the idea of taking a photo of the scene.

'One does not have eyesight. Well that's all,' Kamala continued. 'Each one may have different deficiencies. Do you go about distributing alms to all of them? He is not a lesser person for being blind.'

'Oh Kamala, you and your philosophy! Or is it that of the other guy?'

'Nandan never gave alms to anyone. It was his policy.'

'You also don't give. There ends the matter, ok?'

Kamala sat in silence on the floor of the hall in the temple for quite some time, as if in prayer. She felt that silence was resonating around like a mysterious *mantra.*

They went to a homestay for the night. James had located it the previous night by searching the Internet. A two-storeyed house. Guests on the top floor and superannuated couple on the ground floor. Their children were abroad and they accommodated guests more for companionship than anything else. The rent was comparatively less, as it was not tourist season.

'They are taking us for a couple,' James said, while going up the stairs.

'You could have corrected them.'

'What if they asked us to leave? Where could we go in the night? He asked me to take good care of the wife. And also that the railings of the balcony are low and that she should not be allowed to step out alone.'

'Don't worry. I'm not going out of the room.'

'I'm now a hero for them,' James said.

'Yes, have you not provided a new life to a poor blind person?' Kamala laughed.

James got one more call before they went to bed. He terminated the call without bothering to find out who the caller was and put his cell phone on silent mode.

Kamala was still thinking about the Buddha temple. Last time they had spent most of the day there. They went around the temple premises. The Tibetan art work in the hall, the calligraphy of sacred chants on the walls ... Nandan explained everything to her. The intermittent sound of the lamas praying clanging the bell ... Nandan read out from a board about the traditional lama lineage. Then they had sat in the prayer room in silence for a long while. Kamala was immersed in memories. Slowly she closed her eyes.

'Hey, have you slept?' Kamala opened her eyes feeling his touch on her forehead. Short and rough hands.

'James, you had drinks, no?'

'Just one,' said James, 'for a boost.'

'I don't like it,' said Kamala. 'Nothing goes right if you are drunk.'

'Just for the heck of it. Elizabeth was not like this. Once in a while we used to drink together.'

'It is not drinking as such. If you drink, I would feel that it is alcohol lying with me. As if another person is present in the room.'

'Doesn't matter,' James held her close.

'Don't hold me so tight, James. It hurts me.'

He was in a frenzy. When he pressed her neck, she coughed, unable to breathe. James did not like that.

He imagined that he was making a tour of her body. Waterfalls, lakes, the ups and downs. She turned away when he attempted to kiss her on the cheeks.

'You smell of liquor,' Kamala said. James withdrew his face suddenly.

'You are not cooperating, Kamala,' he said. 'Was it for this that we came all this distance?'

She embraced him as if to console him. It reminded him of the cold he felt when her hands touched him on the path near the waterfall, in the evening.

'Elizabeth called again, isn't it,' Kamala asked.

'She is mad.'

'Forget it James. Why are you so adamant? After all she was with you for quite some time, no?'

'Shit!' James lifted Kamala away from his embrace.

'She used to like you, I know. Is that not enough? Is it a must that she likes only one person for all times to come?'

'Oh, I have never bothered to like her to that extent. She was such a bitch.'

James lit a cigarette. Halfway through he put it out and massaged her arms, perhaps making a second attempt.

He felt something sticking out on her right arm, below the shoulder.

'What is it?'

'Oh, that,' Kamala said, 'a steel rod.'

'What happened?'

'An accident. It is ok,' Kamala felt her right arm with her left. 'That was why I asked you to hold me softly. It hurts even now, though years have passed.'

'When did it happen?'

'Quite some time ago,' Kamala said casually.

'Is it not time to get it out?'

'Yes, I think so. But no. It is a remembrance, no James? Let it remain there.'

James unhooked her nightdress. They went nude with the lights on. Kamala softly kissed his forehead. Then she sat up in the bed.

'Look at my breast,' Kamala asked, as if throwing an invitation. 'There is a mole with a light red tint, no?'

'Where?'

'Here … below the left breast, close to the heart…'

'I will not believe anymore Kamala, that you can't see,' James said pressing his lips on the mole.'

'I didn't know,' Kamala laughed.

'Then? Oh, Nandan must have told you, no?' James ridiculed her.

'For once you have guessed it right,' Kamala said.

For whatever reasons, for the first time James felt the presence of Nandan near him. He went cold.

'Not only that, he even knew the climates of my body … rain and mist and warmth in the real sense. Take a look at my nipples, James. They must be just black now, isn't it?'

'So?'

'I don't have the mood, James. Didn't I tell you? When I'm in the mood for it, my nipples will turn red,' Kamala laughed.

James once again suspected the presence of Nandan. He felt he was losing out to Nandan even though he was invisible. He dragged her close with a vengeance. It was almost an assault. Kamala abided his force, in silence. She felt a honeybee buzzing around her head. His ravenous hunger subsided and she became aware he was lying exhausted on the other side. A roaring silence pierced her and she slipped into sleep.

On waking up, Kamala became aware that she was naked. She probed with her hands and put on her nightdress. The voice of James boomed, may be from the balcony. He was arguing through his phone. Then she heard him hurrying down the stairs.

She did not go out of the room till noon. A girl brought her breakfast and kept it on the table. But she did not touch it.

James showed up at noon.

'You didn't have breakfast,' he asked.

'I didn't feel hungry.'

'Have a bath. We will go out after lunch.'

'Where to?'

'Thalakaveri,' he said. 'That cab will come.'

'No,' said Kamala. 'I don't feel well.'

'Okay, let's not go then. But come and have some food.'

'Not hungry,' she repeated.

'Feverish?'

'No.'

'Then?'

'Then, then, then nothing. Just leave me alone.'

'No wonder he divorced you,' James exploded.

Kamala writhed.

'Who?' Kamala shook herself up. 'Who divorced me, James? Who told you this rubbish?'

'Oh, should I tell you that? Have you not been repeating that name like a mantra all the while?'

Kamala broke into tears. Neither spoke for some time.

'James, let's go for lunch,' Kamala said dabbing her face with a towel. They ate their lunch in silence.

In the afternoon they started off to Mangalore in the taxi. The taxi was passing through an uninterrupted row of dry villages.

'James,' Kamala beckoned. 'I'm sorry. Was I rude to you?'

'Oh, no,' James replied languidly.

'Yes, I know. But … but certain things cannot be changed. Like the steel rod, it is always there in me.'

'Ours was a unique relationship, James. "Made for each other," you had said. That was it. We had made a secret pact that there won't be any regrets even if our relationship is broken. That's why I came with you, made this tour with you. But I think I cannot just handle this role.'

'Leave it,' James said.

'No, it is something else. You asked me why he left me. It was a secret till now. I've not mentioned it to anyone. Not even to friends in Mangalore. I never wanted anybody's sympathy. There's already my blindness for people to sympathise. I'm fed up with that as it is. To add the status of a widow to it … no, I can't stand it.'

'Kamala, what did you say? Widow?'

'That is the truth. Nandan is no more. That is me, a widow. I'm that too now.'

James held her hands. He was again surprised by the chill.

The vehicle carried on ahead at more or less uniform speed through hillocks and dales.

'Kaveri originates from a little spring, isn't it?' Kamala said in a low tone. 'And then it provides water to ever so many villages and towns, irrigates myriad farm lands. It is really a miracle, James. My stupid obstinacy! We could've gone to Thalakaveri.'

'Doesn't matter, we can make it another time,' said James.

'Last time we went there, we sat on the raised platform down below for a while,' Kamala recalled. 'A cool breeze was blowing. A little girl came and sat by our side. Nandan took a snap of hers. I've kept it framed in my room. It is still there. Have you noticed it?'

James did not answer.

'James, you have taken photos of our tour no?' Kamala enquired. 'Where is its card?'

'It is in the camera,' James said. 'We will take prints at Mangalore.'

'What do I need the prints for? You show me the card. Let me touch and feel it.'

He took the camera, extracted the data card and placed it in her palm.

Stunning him, Kamala put it in her mouth and chewed it. Then she opened the door and spat it out.

'Are you mad Kamala? All those pictures are gone, no?' James loudly asked.

'Let it go,' she said very casually.

James looked out. The car was approaching a small town. The traffic's intensity increased.

'Bastard, you took my pictures when I was sleeping, no?' Kamala asked. 'You caught me naked. I had guessed that.'

James looked at her carefully. Those white eye balls … the light from them … that may hurt, he was afraid.

Kamala laughed loudly. 'You can't blackmail a blind person. Never! For a blind person, nudity is in her mind. Still, I don't want those pictures to be in your possession. You are not worthy enough to keep them. You are just a big … big bastard.'

James wiped his face with his hands. And then he looked out.

Now the cab was moving through a one-way traffic lane. A long line of vehicles was ahead of them, blaring horns and other traffic sounds. The car stopped intermittently and rolled forward again. After crawling like that for some more time, it stopped at a signal.

'Look at that signal, James,' Kamala said.

James looked at it.

'You see those digits? Read it. How much time will we be held up at this traffic signal?'

'Another 84 seconds,' James said slowly, reading the red digits.

~

The Gospel According to the Devil

Shatavari Express, 9.20 a.m., at South Central station. The train was on time.

The train was already moving, by the time I hauled myself in. In the hurry, it took some time to find the reserved seat. The road was chock-a-block with long lines of vehicles. The cab I had taken was moving like an animal trying to escape a trap. By the time it grunted and groaned into the station, the moaning whistle of the train had already been sounded. I had prompted the taxi driver to take me up beyond the parking lot and had rushed with the suitcase. A few more seconds and the train would have gathered momentum.

Things were just not going right, as if in continuation of all that running and scurrying. The coach I had got into was not the right one and the ticket examiner ordered me out of the seat and the coach. 'Berth no 36 is alright, but not in this coach; please go to S-6.' So on to the next coach with the bag, through the swaying vestibule. The bag slipped from my hands as I lifted it on to the upper berth and it fell on the man sitting on the lower berth. Fortunately, he didn't shout and confined his protest to a hard stare.

Collapsing on the seat, I closed my eyes and made a mental review of the morning. It was a journey planned at short notice. The intimation was received only the previous evening. An acquaintance in a travel agency had arranged the ticket. I packed my bag early in the morning. Have I taken all the documents? There is no point in going there without all the necessary documents. I became restless, thinking that all this hurry-burry may have been for nothing. I opened my eyes, hoping all would go well.

The young man sitting opposite me was smiling at me. Who is he? Have I met him earlier? I can't recall. He was dressed in spotless white, in a collarless kurta with long sleeves and worn-out bottoms. He had a broad forehead, sparkling eyes, closely cropped hair and big ears like that of the Buddha sporting silver rings. He was dark complexioned with a muscular body of a yogi. He must have been around 35 years. There seemed to be some sort of magnetism in his eyes.

'You seem to be in a great hurry! Where are you going to?'

I told him my destination.

'That's good. That's where I'm going too,' he said smiling.

If the train is in time, it will reach there by tomorrow evening. Well, it's good to have a talking companion.

'What is your name?' I enquired.

'Kumar,' he said. 'Kumar Sadhu is the full name. You can call me Sadhu.'

'You're a sanyasin?' I asked him, for the name sounded a little strange.

'Only in name,' He laughed. 'I cannot say whether I'll become one in future.'

He did not ask for and nor did I tell him my name.

'You had a tough time, it seems,' he smiled.

'Yes. It was sheer luck. The train had started moving, when I jumped in.'

'You were caught in a traffic snarl, no?' Sadhu had guessed correctly. 'It's strange. The roads are getting wider but the traffic is slowing down.'

I noticed that his words were very soft. He spoke in a low voice, just loud enough for me to hear. His face reflected a deep tranquility.

'You'd have been in trouble had you missed this train, no?' Sadhu asked.

I nodded. Yes, indeed. I would have been in difficulties.

'See, at times we'll have to make direct interventions. Always allowing things to take their course may create complications.' He continued after a pause. 'For example, you should've taken more care to reach the station in time.'

'What could I have done?' I thought. 'I started from home very early. I took a taxi instead of a bus, to save time.'

'It is true that you can't prevent traffic jams,' Sadhu said, as if reading my thoughts.

'But you could've stopped this train from leaving till you reached here.'

'Stopping the train?' I was bewildered.

'Why not? You had made all preparations for this journey. You had reserved your ticket, got ready and out of the house well in time. Still you were caught in the traffic. And that traffic block was not of your creation. So what else can you do other than delaying the departure of the train?'

A passenger reaching the platform just as the signal has turned green, will he try to board the train or block it? What is this guy trying to say?

'No, no. It was before that you had to act,' he continued with an air of detachment. 'There's no point in waiting till you reach the station. Anyway it'd be too late.'

What action is he referring to?

'Nothing much. Get into a busy telephone booth and make a local call. That's all.'

'And whom do I call?'

'The police. That's easier. If you call the railway, they will then have to contact the police. That is a roundabout way.'

I just could not understand what he meant.

'See, what is it that you want? The train should be detained for some time, isn't it? The need is yours. But there are certain obstacles not of your creation. So get rid of them.'

'So?'

'This is such a trifle these days, even kids would understand. Just say that a bomb has been planted in this train. How easy! By the time the police and their dogs complete the search, you could leisurely reach the station. But you have to be careful. A busy telephone booth, it is very important. No one should notice you. Another thing, you should not be hurrying when you reach the station. It should be as if you got the train quite accidentally. As a precaution, it would be better if you don't go to the seat you had booked.'

This man, who appeared to be of sober disposition, was discussing desperate and risky things. At the same time I found him nonchalantly looking out of the window. He seemed not at all bothered about our conversation being overheard by others.

It was a fast train and stopped at few stations. The others except Sadhu were sleeping. I too dozed off, leaning on my seat.

The train was at a busy station when I woke up. 'Which is this station?' Many passengers were getting down on to the platform. A few others were talking on their cell phones, while wandering in the limited perimeter of the coach. Vendors with tea, fruits and water were already in the compartment. An elderly man was being led on a wheel chair by a man and a woman to the next compartment. And the din was dominated by the sounds of trains arriving and leaving on other tracks.

Sadhu was not to be seen. Maybe he has stepped out on to the platform. I too thought of going out, but then a boy with a load of books came in and displayed them on the opposite seat. Old novels, women's magazines, cartoons and illustrated stories for children … I leafed through them and so remained in the coach without going out.

It was an old copy of Gandhi's *My Experiments with Truth* that I bought from him. I got it quite cheap. It would be good if the kids read it, I thought. The train was moving by the time I was through the first page.

I closed the book after reading the first few pages of the preface. I had a mild headache. Sadhu was right there on the opposite seat, sitting cross-legged and lost in the sights outside. I had almost forgotten him, engrossed in the book.

'*My Experiments with Truth*, do you want to take a look?' I asked, extending it to him.

'I saw it.' He did not take the book from me. 'Maybe, you bought it for your children?'

I nodded. 'But it is certainly a book that can be read by the grown-ups too. Many may have only heard of it and not read it. Like me.'

'If it is out of concern for the children's future, I'd say that such books do not serve much purpose,' Sadhu continued with a smile. 'Not only that, reading such moralistic stories would only harm rather than benefit them.'

'Why do you say so?' I argued. 'Gandhi's books are bound to do good for the children. I have never heard a contrary opinion.'

Sadhu was silent for few seconds. Then he said, 'Please look at the blurb on the back cover. What does it say?'

I turned the book around and started reading. 'Truth and non-violence have been there since long. They are as old as the mountains. That's what it says, no?'

'Yes. And is it not correct?' I asked. But there was no response from Sadhu.

After a long silence, he started speaking as if in continuation.

'Well, such good ideas to be presented to children! But to what kind of a world are you sending your children? Do you expect them to live there with mutual respect and in peaceful coexistence? If so, moral lessons and right paths are all okay. However, what is going to happen in reality?'

I had absolutely no inkling of what Sadhu was hinting at.

'Do you really think those are the times they will be living in? They live in a world of intense competition. Chances are that it will increase manifold in future. Defeat of the other is one's endeavour in that world. In fact, are you not just flinging your children into the den of violent animals? Only the fall of one will create space for another to have a foothold. Is it based on truth and justice that this world is moving ahead? Do you think that our society is following those ideals? Or has it ever done so? In which case, you tell me of what use are such books and moral teachings?'

'Then what kind of books do you suggest?' I was peeved at him. There are some people who always come out against anything and everything. Sadhu seemed to be one of them.

'You are disturbed by what I said?' he smiled. 'You please continue with your reading. I've read it some time ago. These were only a few general observations.'

But I did not read any more and instead was happy looking out of the window. Some of my co-passengers unpacked the food packets they had brought with them. I was not carrying any food but then got a packet from the caterers.

I noticed that Sadhu was not having any lunch. Before I started eating I enquired: 'No lunch?'

'No, I don't usually eat anything from outside.' He took out a plantain from his shoulder bag and took a sip of water from his water bottle.

'Just this?'

'Enough and more. Hunger is a state of mind, no?' he asked, to my amusement.

The train sped past deserted landscapes. Cacti had taken over farmlands left fallow. That uni-dimensional scene persisted for quite some distance. Not a human being was to be seen. The train passed through several small bridges. The rivers and streams below the bridges were all dry. May be because of Sadhu's lecture, I did not feel like reading *My Experiments with Truth*, sitting right in front of him. His words had indeed made an impact on me, even though it was a little one. Viewed from one perspective, there was some substance in what he said. The humans were all rushing and running without any specific destinations. No time for anyone to look at or think about anyone else. What utility value is there for morals and wise lessons in the midst of all this? But what else can be done, will be the counterargument. There ought to be books, which would be of help to people in a future driven by competition and mad rush. Which is that book? Where will that be available?

'I've a feeling that such a book exists. It must be there somewhere. And if it is not there, it will not be long before it is written,' Sadhu said, as if divining my thoughts.

'Wonderful! Does he have mind-reading abilities?' I looked at him with bewilderment, but his response was a cool smile. The train had slowed down. A station, I presumed.

'There could be a "Devil's Gospel". The possibility of that is very high,' Sadhu said.

'A "Devil's Gospel?"'

'Or something with a similar name. There is bound to be a book of that kind capable of leading this world into the future. But if you do some hard thinking, can you give it any name other than the *Devil's Gospel*?'

He was certainly not expecting any response from me.

A few minutes later, the train reached a station neither too small nor big. However, it had no halt there, so it reduced its speed, had a look at the station and then sped away. Those on the platform seemed to gape at the speeding train, as if in awe of the long-distance travellers.

'In fact I've been on the hunt for it, for quite some time,' Sadhu continued from where he had left off. 'The *Devil's Gospel*, but so far it has eluded my grasp.'

'Where do you search for it?' I was curious.

'I'm proceeding on assumptions. Certain individuals, organisations, even certain communities … I'm sure they will be in possession of it. Their working style and methods are indications to that. Otherwise how could they carry on without a wrong step and with such confidence? I've spent some time on them and so I can say with certainty that they have the book with them. But I'm not getting hold of it. That's why these days…' He stopped and took out a water bottle from his shoulder bag and had a gulp.

'These days I've been thinking about the content of such a book. What would be the topics? What kind of experiences will be highlighted in it? Or what would be its style … On the whole, I've been in deep thought about it. In the background of my contemplations and my experiences to date, the chances are that my conjecture is quite accurate."

'Can you explain…?'

"Suppose, that book comes my way at some point of time in life, there couldn't be anything in it that I'd not have thought of. Because it is impossible to inscribe the *Devil's Gospel* in any other manner.

I was not getting the full sense of what he was trying to tell. Talking about a book merely based on conjectures, to visualise it, predict that that book will get to him sometime in the future … and also to have clear ideas about its contents. This was all beyond me.

'I think so much about the content and the format of the book that at times I feel I might be the one to write it.'

And then Sadhu laughed out loud and long. Throughout he was smiling or laughing, but I hadn't seen him laugh like this. However, it was as soft as the smooth flow of a stream. He became absolutely calm afterwards. The furrows on his forehead had vanished.

As night fell, I opened my suitcase, took out the mineral water bottle to which some vodka had been added and had a couple of swigs. All the while I did not glance even once in Sadhu's direction. When travelling long distances, I had this habit of carrying some liquor with me to overcome boredom. And if it was vodka, chances of others noticing it too was quite remote.

'You must lock your suitcase and also secure it with a chain,' Sadhu reminded me, as we were about to turn in for the night. 'A train coach after all, no? Can't say who all may come in and who all may get out as we sleep.'

'I don't have a chain with me. Forgot to pack it.'

'Oh, that's risky. You are carrying money and documents, no? Have to be vigilant.' He then dug into his shoulder bag and came up with a chain and lock. He helped me to fasten the chain to the hook underneath the seat and handed over the key to me. His chain, his lock and now he was giving me the key … I hesitated.

'No, no. you should keep the key. It is not very prudent to trust a stranger,' he said.

I laughed, accepting the key from him.

'That is a lesson,' Sadhu said, laughing along with me. 'That is a very important lesson in the *Devil's Gospel.* "Don't trust anyone." Perhaps that could be the very first chapter.' Then he told me in a hush-hush tone. 'Another thing is not to drink, when you are in such an alien setting. Liquor will block our rationality, even if temporarily.' I was astounded. This man sees all.

'I don't mean that one should be anti-alcohol. Liquor and intoxication have vital possibilities in the gospel I was talking about. That could be of use to you as a tool in critical situations,' he continued. 'Those who have understood what alcohol really is, do not drink. They will instead induce others to drink. If at all they drink, it will be for tempting the other and trapping him.'

I lay down on the berth, going over all that he had said. The lurching and jolting of the train was too much at times. Light beams from the stations that we passed by, peeped into the dark compartment. Sleeping was an off-and-on process. And sometimes it was as if the train had come to a standstill. But being on the upper berth meant no disturbance of any kind. I slowly drifted into slumber.

It was quite bright when I woke up. The train was pushing ahead at great speed. I got down from the berth.

Many of those who had been there the previous evening had vanished and new faces had replaced them. The landscape too had changed. No more greenery. Only fallow farm lands. Yet, there were a few farmers with bullocks and ploughs. Small stations with huddles of parked bicycles. A line of huts for some distance. An air of deprivation and decay.

And now toothbrush and paste. But where is the suitcase? It was not there, where it was kept locked. Kumar Sadhu too was not there on his seat. He had told me that he was also travelling to the same place as I was. What will I do now without the suitcase? Whom shall I complain to if the money and the documents are lost? My restlessness was mounting.

'I shifted the suitcase beneath the seat. We had kept it upright and it was wobbling.' I turned round, upon hearing Sadhu's voice. He had had a bath and was dressed in fresh white clothes. The same calm smile was there on his lips. I felt bad that I had suspected his integrity.

While brushing, I learnt from the conversation among other passengers that the train was running late by four hours. It could be further delayed as there would be some sort of regulated running during the day. I recalled that the train was standing still for quite some time in the night.

'It seems there was a riot on the way. Must have been in the town near the station, where our train was held up. There was a fear that the train could become a target for the rioters,' Sadhu clarified, when I returned to my seat.

'We will be terribly late,' I said.

'There are no alternatives, no?' His face did not betray any anxieties.

'Which was the last station?' The person who was sleeping on the berth opposite to mine looked down and asked. Sadhu looked up towards him and mentioned the name of the station.

'Oh, I'm done for.' He shouted and jumped down and stared through the window, banging his forehead with his hand.

'Were you to get down there?' I asked.

"Yes! The train was scheduled to reach there at four in the morning. Now that the train is delayed, it will be at least seven by the time that station is reached, the conductor had told me. Oh, how terrible!' It seemed, he would cry.

'You can get down at the next station,' I consoled him.

'That won't do. I must reach there by nine. And this damned train will now stop only after another 100 kilometers. What shall I do? Oh God!' I was not getting any ideas that would be of any help to him.

Sadhu stood up. 'Don't worry. We may have travelled another five kilometers, that's all. If you get down here, you can reach your place by nine.'

He instantly pulled the alarm chain and sat down on his seat absolutely unperturbed.

The train slowed down and came to a halt. It was a small village. Urchins grazing cattle stared at the train with wondering eyes. A train standing still so close by must have been a rare sight for them.

'Get down, friend!' Sadhu urged that passenger. 'You must leave before the officials arrive.'

He collected his bags and jumped out and scrambled through the narrow lanes as if someone were in pursuit of him.

Two guards of the train reached the coach shortly. They looked quite annoyed.

'As it is, we are running late. Now what happened?' It was a general question, not addressed to anyone in particular. No one replied.

'Who pulled the chain?' One of the guards raised his voice. Again there was no response.

'A passenger,' Sadhu told them with firmness. 'He just got down and ran away.'

'Damnation! These guys want express trains to stop at their door steps!' They left the coach in agitation. It was quite surprising that no one else in the compartment spoke.

'The riot and arson were not of his making,' Sadhu told me with a chuckle as the train started moving.

The train got delayed further, as I had feared. It slowed down occasionally and was even held back at a few stations to give way to other trains.

The boredom of waiting led to getting acquainted with other passengers. One had a pack of playing cards and we made a makeshift table with suitcases. When one of the players dropped out, Sadhu was invited to make up the quorum. I never expected a person like Sadhu to indulge in cards. But to my surprise, he joined us with enthusiasm.

His style of playing was quite different and also astonishing. Sadhu was slick with the cards. Even as he concentrated hard on his hand, he seemed to be aware of the cards with the others. He kept on winning, but was quite dispassionate about it.

One of the players took out tetrapacks of Frooti from his bag and offered it to others, even as he drank from one.

'I don't drink it,' Sadhu refused the offer. 'I'm of the opinion that no one should accept offers of drinks from co-passengers.'

I had an instinctive feeling that that piece of advice was directed at me. Whatever it be, when I too refused the drink, he tried to lighten the situation by laughing it away as a joke. Maybe this is the second lesson from the *Devil's Gospel* he was talking about the previous day—'Don't accept anything from anyone.'

We continued the card game for some more time. The afternoon crawled along drearily. I whiled away the time sleeping, drinking tea and discussing everything under the sun. It was eleven in the night by the time the train arrived at our station. Almost seven hours late. Bleary-eyed passengers went out into the darkness of the night.

The compartment had practically emptied out. We got down leisurely.

'Where are you headed for?' Sadhu asked me, while helping me to get my suitcase down.

'Girinagar in Kalashpuri,' I said.

'Oh, it must be about 20 kilometres. Will you get a bus this late?'

'I might, up to Kalashpuri…' I said. 'Maybe a long-distance bus passing by.' The old man in the wheelchair, whom I had seen in the train, was being taken to a taxi outside the station by the same couple.

Sadhu came with me to the bus stand, which was about a kilometre away. He helped me with the suitcase, by carrying it for me for some distance. Maybe because of the exhaustion of the journey, I felt the suitcase had become heavier.

The bus stand and the surroundings were quite deserted. Lights did not flicker from any of the parked buses. All the shops in the vicinity were closed. There were no signs of any long distance buses either.

'Shall I try to engage a taxi or a rickshaw?' I asked Sadhu.

'I don't think anyone will take you,' Sadhu was thoughtful. 'And even if someone is ready to drive you there, I'd say that you shouldn't go.'

'Why?'

'You have to go through deserted areas. It's risky. These are not the best of times. Quite often the stories we hear are not very pleasant. Caution will serve us better.' Then he asked me with some hesitation, 'After this kind of discussion it is not very easy for me to ask you to trust me. However, will it not be better if you stay at my place tonight?'

I looked at his face. The same calmness as always. Moreover I had no alternative.

We returned by the same road. There were a few people near the railway station even at that time of night. But, thereafter, it was all deserted roads and lonesomeness. It was a cloudy night. There were several lamp posts, but few had bulbs burning. It was like walking through a zone of shadows.

But Sadhu was quite familiar with the place. He was walking with firm steps, as if traversing through a well-lit road. I had to struggle to keep pace with him. The road gave way to narrow lanes. Sadhu took over my suitcase.

While stumbling through a one-foot track by the edges of a massive building complex, he turned around and cautioned me: 'Be careful. One wrong step and you will fall into the canal. It is the sewage from this building. It is quite deep.'

He waited till I caught up with him. Taking my palm he led the way.

'Where pray, this man is taking me through this dirty sewage?' The indications he had given me during the journey and the reference to the *Devil's Gospel* crowded my mind. I was scared.

A pack of stray dogs came barking down on us. Sadhu stopped and raised his hand at the bounding dogs. The barking stopped. They retreated howling, as if from a severe blow. The whole thing was so eerie.

We reached a small bridge after walking for some more time. The bridge connected the vast sewage area with the rest of the earth on the other side. The stench from the sewage was overpowering. It seemed to follow us as we reached a row of small houses in a straight single line. All of them had tin roofs. They were all closed from inside. There were no lights anywhere. One could make out people sleeping huddled together on the verandas.

Sadhu put down the suitcase, took out a key from his shoulder bag and opened the lock on the door of a room.

He unbolted the door. The sound of iron scratching on the wooden door made a strange effect in the darkness of the night.

One of the sleeping figures woke and jumped up. Recognising Sadhu, he moved to a side with bent head. He had tattered clothes, unkempt hair and a beard. He seemed to be a beggar.

'Go back to sleep. I'm slightly late,' Sadhu said as he stepped into the room.

Sadhu switched on the light and invited me to sit on the coir cot. It was a small room. There was a small table and chair near a window, which was closed. There was a folded mat under the cot. Some vessels in a corner and few pots hung on the nails on the wall. The rest of the space in the room was occupied by books. Books, old and new, periodicals, diaries, written notes…

'Will it be okay if you have your bath in the morning?' Sadhu asked. 'I know you are tired and a bath will make you feel fresh. But very little water is available now. Maybe we can use it for making some food.' He went out without waiting for my answer, taking a small vessel with him. There were feeble sounds of water falling into the vessel from a tap. I went through the books and the notes, which were scribbled in a hand I was unable to decipher.

'They are all complaints and petitions I prepared for various people,' Sadhu said. He obviously saw me scanning through the notes. But he did not seem to have any objection to that. But I was slightly embarrassed on being caught peeping at what could have been personal papers.

Sadhu lit the stove and put the water to boil. The smell of kerosene filled the room. He sat down on the floor and kneaded the dough for making *rotis*. He sliced potatoes and made a curry. The dinner was ready in minutes. We spread the mat and sat down to eat.

'So many books and papers … What kind of work are you engaged in?' I asked.

'I cannot specify my work. I do all kinds of work,' Sadhu was obviously evading an answer. I recalled his telling a fellow card player that he was on the lookout for a job.

Dinner over, Sadhu took out a fresh sheet and spread it on the coir cot. 'You can sleep here,' he told me. 'I've some more work to finish. My plans have been upset because of the late arrival of the train. I'm not sure if I can complete it or if I can postpone it to tomorrow morning.'

He removed the books from the table and stacked them on the floor. Opening the window, he took out a writing board and papers and started writing.

'You are busy with the book you mentioned about, no?' I asked him, recalling our conversations in the train.

He gave me a blank stare.

'That book. The *Devil's Gospel…*'

Sadhu just laughed and did not comment.

'You may switch off the light. It is just below the calendar. I've a table lamp here,' he said.

I got up and walked in the direction he pointed, but could not locate the switch. I glanced at the calendar and found that Sadhu had made notes—places, persons, etc., below most of the dates. Maybe it was his programme chart. I lifted the calendar and found a framed photograph. A fading black and white picture of a rustic man and woman. An elderly couple. One could discern a faint resemblance of Sadhu on the man's face.

'Your father and mother?' I enquired. Sadhu, who was busy writing with bent head, turned around and nodded and went back to writing.

'Where are they?' I asked.

'Nowhere. Both of them are dead,' he continued, without raising his head. "That photo was taken after they were dead. You can make out that if you take a close look at it.'

A picture taken after death being displayed on the wall … I thought it strange.

'There were no earlier photos...' Sadhu said, as if to dispel my doubts.

'Did they die together? But how could that happen? Suicide?'

'They were shot dead,' Sadhu said. He did not raise his head from his writing board.

'By whom?' I asked anxiously.

'The police. There was a riot in the town that day,' Sadhu's tone did not betray any emotions.

I switched off the light.

All that remained was the bent head of Sadhu in the spherical light of the table lamp, like a framed picture.

The tedious train journey and exhaustion quickly took me to sleep. When I woke up once, I saw that the table lamp was still on. Sadhu was immersed in his work. I changed sides and drifted to sleep.

I woke up again after some time. But this time it was completely dark. I didn't know what the time was. I stared into the darkness.

After I got used to the darkness, I looked around. There was no sign of Sadhu. He was not to be seen anywhere. I got up from the cot.

Something struck my feet. I bent down.

He was fast asleep on the mat, on his back. With his left arm tucked under his head like a pillow. His face was as tranquil as that of a yogi.

I walked up to the table without making any noise. The writing board was stacked with written papers.

I looked out through the small window. In the dull light of the street lights, I could see the narrow streets we had trudged through the previous night. Beyond there were the skyscrapers, the sewage canal, the bridge, the row of small shops, rickshaws parked on the streets and small vehicles. It looked like the margins of the city.

And silence was all pervading.

In that mystifying silence, under the gloomy light of the skies, I witnessed the world sleeping, like a tattered book.

~

My Father was a Thief

Have you ever been out fishing with a line and hook when you were young? Do you recall the first time you hooked a fish. Don't you even today feel the urgency with which the dry twig, which was till now lying on the water like a dead body, plunged deep down? And also the frantic writhing at the other end to escape from the hook as you pull the line?

On all such occasions, the fish were tugging at the line of their life. And in most cases, they lost those treacherous contests.

Some memories are like that. They linger without fading. For me it is all there as if it happened yesterday—digging out and separating the earthworms, which were entwined like nude bodies. Keeping them in a leaf-bowl, fixing the hook at one end of the line and tying it to a sturdy stick, making a float out of a dry twig...

How can I ever forget all that?

The fish I caught that day was very small. One of its eyes had come loose. Maybe the hook had pierced the eye. That eye seemed to shine in a groovy green colour in the daylight. Blood had drained out and the cavity where the eye was, had become pale. The fish writhed and jumped up when it was released from the hook. A terrible dance for clutching on to life. Boys, my neighbours in the line-rooms, made a ruckus, banging empty tins with sticks, jumping up and down imitating the little fish. They were celebrating as if they had won a trophy. But by then the excitement of catching the fish had oozed out from me. The sight of a tiny nerve, starting from the half fallen eye like a slender red river saddened me. I got an abandoned glass jar from the heap of wires and other rubbish left by telephone-cable workers. Its edges were broken. I filled it with water and let the fish swim in it. After probing the depth of the jar, the little fish surfaced and remained there touching the glass with its lips. It was trying to listen to something, I felt. The water in the jar was lukewarm from the noon sun.

It was the day before the saint's festival. It is fresh in my mind. Ma had gone early in the morning to the church to work on the temporary stage that was being constructed for the next day's festivities. All the grown-ups, who lived in the line-rooms, had found work there. The occupant of the last room, one-eyed Achu, alone did not go. He never went anywhere. He had only a shallow hole where his left eye should have been. Achu had a kerosene lamp in front him and he was lighting the leftover crackers of the last Vishu festival. Slowly taking out the crackers from a cloth bag, he was allowing a considerable time gap between one burst and the next, all the while panting like a mad dog. The long silence between one bang and the next was intolerable. As if the dread of the coming explosion was hanging around. But Achu was unmindful of all that. Since he had only one eye, I always felt that he was taking aim at someone, whenever he was looking in any direction. I took care not to look at him as I passed the courtyard with the glass jar. Whenever I glanced at the fish in the jar, I would remember the single eye of Achu. I had never seen him smile, just as was the case with the fish.

Opening the two-panelled door of the house, I placed the jar in a corner. The little fish was standing still at the water's surface. Its gills were moving slightly. The point just below the gills, where the hook had gone in had become a red scar.

I minced the earthworms, which were left in the leaf-bowl and put them into the jar. But the fish hardly stirred. Bang! One of Achu's crackers startled me.

Yes, how can I forget? It was that night my father returned home after a long absence.

Darkness had thickened. Ma was lying in a corner of the room exhausted by the day's work. Supper was not yet over. Light from the lone bulb was insufficient for the room. Darkness was reluctant to leave. I sat silent leaning on the dirty wall, the shadow of one defeated. I didn't want to look at the glass jar.

Someone knocking on the door. When it was repeated, I went up the veranda and opened it. It took me no time to recognise the lean and lanky figure standing in the dim light: my father. Despite sporting a mustache and the two scars on the forehead, Pa resembled me. But his eyes had sunk deep. His hair was unkempt. 'Not growing up?' he asked smiling, displaying his broken front teeth. His sound was dry and tuneless and came out from some other body, I felt. I did not answer him. Someone in the other room coughed and spat out loudly. The smell of arrack invaded the room as Pa came in.

My father was a thief. I've no problem in confessing this. All our neighbours knew. The boys who came cow-grazing on the banks of the river, teased me whenever I went to play in the open ground, where the telephone workers dump their things. But I always ignored them. They were talking about someone else, I'd think. I never used to feel anything whenever there was any talk of my father. He had left home long ago and had not so far been a part of my life.

Ma came to the front of the room hearing pa speak. The expressions on her tired face were not clear to me in the shadowed light of the room. Her face was anyway not suited for sadness. 'Released?' she queried. I could see him winking 'no'.

'And then?'

'Was in hospital for four days,' he said. 'And then I sneaked away from there.'

'You could've completed your term.'

Ma raised her voice, 'Will they leave you alone now, if they get hold of you?'

Pa asked her to keep her volume down. 'It would've meant two more years there.'

'Won't they come here searching for you?'

'What of it? I'm leaving early in the morning.'

'Back to jail?'

'No, I have managed a job in the forests. Lumbering.'

'I know for sure that you can't make a living by working.' Ma never trusted Pa. 'Is there any bone intact in your body, with all the thrashing you get from the police?'

'You just wait and watch. I've given up that kind of life.'

'But wherever you go, the police will come for you, no?'

'Only if they find out where I am, no?' Pa said. 'Last time they got me because someone squealed on me. Don't you tell anyone that I'd been here.' He then turned towards me as if in an afterthought. 'Will you tell anyone?'

I didn't answer him.

'Doesn't he talk at all?' Pa asked Ma, while glaring at me.

She was busy serving me food and didn't seem to hear him.

I ate silently with my eyes fixed on the plate. I stole a look at Pa. He was leaning back on the floor and was staring at me. I was upset. I was in such a hurry to finish the meal that rice was strewn all over the floor, around the plate.

'What's in that?' It was only then Pa noticed the glass jar in the corner of the room. Ma just glanced at it but did not reply.

'What's in it?' He asked me after few minutes. He was still keeping his voice low.

'Fish,' I said with hesitation.

'Fish?' Pa stretched his hand and took up the jar. He was not very careful with it and some water spilled over.

'It is dead,' he said as if teasing me. It was indeed lying supine in the water. Slightly bloated too, I felt. The sparkle in the split eye had vanished.

'Where did you get this little one from?' The broken front teeth were all too visible, when he laughed.

'I caught it from the river,' I said. The fish was with me since morning. I was very sad that it had died.

'Are there fish in the river?' Pa asked ma.

'How do I know?' She was angry. 'If I spend my time on all that, how will there be anything to eat in this house?'

Pa was silent for sometime. Then he slowly got up from the floor. Dry fish being fried in one of the nearby rooms. Pa stood close to the wall trying to breathe in the strong smell.

'I've some work,' Pa said. 'Is there a piece of wire in this house?' he asked Ma.

She went inside carrying my plate, without replying.

There was a sound of a cracker from outside.

'Who is bursting crackers at this time of night?' Pa asked with scorn.

'Achu,' I said slowly.

'Achu? Who is this Achu? Oh, that one-eyed fellow? He is not yet dead? I'll pluck his fuse, if he cracks another one, you tell him.'

I was terrified of Achu and was surprised hearing Pa speak, as if he didn't know anything about Achu.

'Achu, yes, okay. He'll have the wire.' Pa thought for a while. 'You go and ask him for a piece of wire.' Then he whispered into my ear, furtively, 'You may tell him that it is for me. He is a wretched fellow, but harmless. He won't tell anyone.'

I knocked on Achu's door, with trepidation.

When he opened the door, the smell of smoke from the kerosene lamp and gunpowder hit my nostrils. The crackers were almost over. The empty bag lay on the floor like a wet animal.

Achu looked at me with his one eye, as if taking aim. He was breathing hard. I asked him for the wire, as Pa had told me to.

'Oh, Mathukkutty is here?' He asked, without showing any surprise and went in. He was back instantly with a roll of wire.

'There is nothing Achu doesn't have with him,' Pa commented with glee. 'He doesn't really need two eyes.'

Are you going out fishing at this time of night?' Ma did not hide her anger.

'You close the door, I'll be back soon.' Then he turned towards me and asked, 'The Melamuri family has a pump-house on the river no?'

'Yes,' I nodded.

'Melamuri Pappachan waters his coconut trees daily, no?'

I nodded again.

I wake up daily hearing the hum of the motor switched on by Melamuri Pappachan to water his coconut and areca nut trees.

'My limbs get excited when I see a coconut tree full of nuts. That's still a problem with me,' Pa said more to himself, stepping out of the room.

A while after Pa left, as if he woke up from a reverie, Achu burst two crackers. The walls of the room seemed to tremble from the impact of the sound. I felt that even the gills of the dead fish in the jar moved.

'He went away … the demon,' cursed Ma next morning. 'I should've known better than to wait for him. He must have gone to rob someone.'

'Oh God, I don't understand, did he come here just to starve me of my supper yesterday?' she continued in frustration. She threw away the fish in the pot. It occurred to me then that I had forgotten the line and hook on the riverbank the previous day.

One of the Saint's Day, processions from the church passed by on the river's shore. A band set dressed in white shirts and red caps accompanied the procession. They were playing popular tunes heard in the cinema halls. The urchins of the colony danced to the tunes, least bothered about any rhythm. Grown-up children led the procession, holding huge umbrellas of various hues. As the procession passed the line-rooms, a couple of youths burst a string of crackers holding them in their hands. One after the other, it seemed the sound and flashes of the crackers would never end. Through the window I could see Achu looking on from his room, as the crackers soared up in the air. A strange kind of silence pervaded when everything was over. The air was filled with thick white smoke. A few seconds later a small boy feebly blew a horn, piercing the silence.

There will be many such processions coming to the church from various localities. I didn't go to the church despite Ma urging me.

The next day two policemen visited all the line-rooms. They looked at me sharply, but didn't ask anything. One of them poked at the rolled-up mats with his stick. Achu was slyly following them with his one eye, till they were out of sight.

On the third day of the Saint's Day celebrations, Pa's dead body was sighted among the screw-pine shrubs in the river. A crowd pulled it on to the shore. It lay on the wet shore like a big stranded fish. The body was bloated, maybe from drinking too much of water. Burnt rolls of wire entangled his neck like a snake. The wounds on his legs from the screw-pine thorns had the colour of rotten flesh.

I didn't go near Pa. I was apprehensive that fish in the river may have bitten off his eyes.

Death Game

We had to advance the date we had fixed for 'finishing' Kontha Shaji. There was this news that he was going to a meditation center for two weeks' prayers. Not for nothing is he called *Kontha*, rosary! It may even be a month by the time he returns after attaining salvation. I can't afford to wait till then. And then Kocha's parole was nearly over and he has to get back. He is a must for this entertainment. It will have more vigour if he joins us.

Together we had finished off Punnose Thampi, something like six years ago. It was Kontha Shaji, who had informed us of his whereabouts. Then too, Kontha had this irritating 'divine call' problem. He will not touch a knife, sword or bomb. But he is a born-snake and venomous too. Treachery is his line. He informed on Punnose Thampi, who was his mentor. Even at death, Thampi would not have known that it was Kontha who had betrayed him. A top-class operator.

Even after diluting the case to the maximum, Kocha and I got a sentence of three and five years respectively. Kontha turned approver. He had come twice to the jail to see us. He would talk to us only about the Word, the path of the Cross and the Last Judgment. We understood his trick. Next time he gets it, we had decided. But he never turned up since.

Poothalingan Chetty, whose finance company had gone bankrupt, had asked us only to beat up Thampi. But even after a good thrashing, his tusk and trunk were still up. He was challenging us despite a broken leg! Thampi is a king when it comes to insolence. We had turned back, ignoring his tantrums. Then he started abusing our Guru. How was the master to be blamed? Had he not already returned to dust? This Thampi too had for some time licked the crumbs that Guru doled out. I cannot let go anyone off, why, not even my own father, if he insults the one who gave me bread and butter. Kocha kicked just once. The shriek that followed must've shattered the horizon. Thampi prone on the broken cement floor had shrivelled like a centipede. All of his bitches from the Chakkanthara colony kicked off their bed rags and came running. Almost a hundred of them, eunuch-like rag tags. The scum would tear us into pieces, if we wavered even slightly. 'Out with the knife', I shouted at Kocha. I walked in front, my dagger held high, its tip shining in the dark, as if nothing has happened. Kocha is really an ass, in a sense. He goes to the movies too frequently. He was cracking some of those filmy dialogues following me with the drawn knife. We marched like that up to the end of the shit-smelling alley passing through Chakkanthara colony. The norm is that we should not panic or show any urgency, even if we over-stepped our task. That's what we learnt from the expeditions with our Guru. Kocha folded the knife and started the Yezdi, which was parked on the side. He had to kick several times, before it started. I kept the crowd at bay, at dagger point, till Kocha turned the bike. As we moved along, those women cannibals of the colony started hurling choice abuses at us that would've made even hell blush. 'Go you whores, to the son of a bitch lying there, half dead,' we slowed down the bike and shouted at them. 'Start moaning instead of chanting your fucking lullabies.' The women of that colony have very little experience of wailing. Death or birth or life, it's always mayhem. It's those stinking songs, be it Easter or Good Friday. Suddenly Kontha, the informer, was sighted. He was crouching at the third turn on the road. The betrayer's shudder never left him.

'Don't stand here, Shaji. Things messed up,' Kocha explained what happened to Thampi. Kontha started bobbing up and down as if in hysteria, clutching and kissing the cross that was hanging on the black thread around his neck. I felt like slapping him on his face. He was sweating profusely. By that time Kocha had come out with a dialogue of his. Disgusted with both of them, I slowly walked to a place, where arrack was available even at that time of night.

It was from there that the police nabbed me. I heard that Punnose Thampi had croaked before reaching the hospital. The police had a go at Kocha. But they did not touch me because they've known me for long. I get a special consideration in the jail too. I don't pick up quarrels with them. They are only doing their work. They have certain faith in me. 'Now that you are leaving, to whom will we handover the kitchen?' the superintendent had once asked me. Flattery of course, but there was some truth in it.

Okay, that was that. Three years went by. Only after coming out free, I came to know of Kontha's latest. Couldn't stomach it, at first. That Kontha Shaji has given up all business. That he is now engaged in spreading the Word. He has married, has a child and built a good house. And the woman he married? None other than the sister of Punnose Thampi! Is he a Satan or a Messiah? But I saw through his game. Thampi had extracted a whole lot of money from the Tamilian moneylenders of the town. Now all of it belongs to Shaji and the gospel mongering is a mere cover-up drama. I really wanted to go and meet him. I don't do anything in a hurry. He is spreading the Word of God, isn't he? What's wrong in a poor fellow like me visiting the holy soul?

When I telephoned, I was told that he has gone to Potta, the Divine Centre. It must've been Thampi's sister who picked up the receiver. I didn't bother to tell her who I was. Just gave her my cell number. I didn't really expect the 'holy man' to return the call, but towards midnight Kontha started singing on my mobile. That call came when I was sitting aimlessly in a dimly lit bar, where everyone else was either too drunk or wallowing in vomit.

I let him know who I was. In a very casual tone. So light.

But he sounded shaky.

'We should meet,' I told him.

He then started rolling about: like 'Oh, why not, any time…'

'I'll come to your home tomorrow,' I said.

'But I'm off to Potta or Muringoor, let's meet another day,' he tried to evade me.

'Tomorrow morning', and I switch off the phone.

Each word has its own value. Bandying words and asking 'How are you?' is not my style. Kontha may have ideas of mobilising and converting a crowd; but I've no such plans whatsoever. And there lies the difference.

But in the morning, the game plan was modified. Why not change the tactics a little? This kind of hide-and-seek is not my way. However, one has to be extra careful when dealing with a person like Kontha. When I reached his home, Kontha was very much there. He had not gone for peddling the Word. Wasn't I sure that he wouldn't go to Potta or anywhere? One end of the unseen noose around his neck is in my hands.

Thampi did not have the good fortune to enjoy the loot from the moneylenders of the town. But his sister and brother-in-law made the best of it. His drawing room was decorated with Virgin Mary as the centrepiece. An ever-burning lamp in front of it. At least four crosses in the drawing room itself. My nerves tingled seeing this showoff. But I didn't say anything.

Thampi's sister started crying the moment she saw me. She used to be such a skinny girl. But she has perked up on the whole, after getting hold of Poothalingan Chetty's money. That's very much visible on her body too. That she cried, I can understand. But that wretch Kontha too starts sobbing! What a great piece of acting! I somehow managed not to laugh.

She went in to make tea and Kontha tried using the interlude for converting me. His good old rhyme of the Word, Sin and Trumpet was heard again. I indulged him and was curious to know to what extent he would go. Then he led me by hand to an inner room. There was enough stuff there for anyone to go insane. He was worshipping a life-size portrait of Thampi!

'Who is this Shaji, dear?' I played the fool. 'Your father eh?'

His eyes welled up even as he emitted a nasal sound. 'What happened that day was a big mistake. We shouldn't have done that to Thampichayan.'

'Really? If so, what about his men threatening us?'

'That was merely a misunderstanding.'

'Thampi had beaten up even your father. Why not a portrait of your father?'

He was silent for quite some time. 'You should forgive me. I've given up everything.'

Given up everything indeed! What about worshipping the photo of the 'Great Guru' Punnose Thampi? Blurting out nonsense is all right, but who the fuck is he to act like this? And who was he in his earlier life? A pimp? An informer?

I would've been softer towards Kontha, had he not staged that stupid drama when I was about to leave. That swindler Thampi's sister enters carrying a brat. I have a casual glance and come down the steps.

'You should bless the child,' Kontha ran down the steps. I could feel the last thread of patience in me snapping. I have to escape before he makes a priest out of me. I somehow controlled myself and was on my way. It takes me only a minute to make any brat cry. A mere look can do the trick. Kontha trying to hoodwink the sorcerer!

I could hear that brat wailing. I didn't turn around.

I felt I'd go mad thinking about him. How could one debase oneself to this extent? That thought did not fade out even after a pint. The times are such that when one takes a conscious decision not to go after these fuckers, they are inviting us to kick their ass. Anyway, there's nothing great in going on like this twirling one's mustache, unless one disposes off at least Kontha's case. It was then that the news of Kocha's parole arrived. Even though a total bore, he's trustworthy. I should involve him before he spoils himself further, watching all those stupid movies.

I was deep in thought about a workable scheme, when luckily, Kontha called me. He was preaching to me even on the mobile: holy words and stories of those who got reformed.

'I too was thinking on your lines,' I sold it to him in a soft tone.

'Praise the lord!' Kontha shouted passionately.

'We should meet…' I said.

'Brother…' he crooned in the style of whores pretending to be in heat.

I made some calculations and told him a date. 'I'll not be alone, Shaji; our Kocha will also be there.' A golden opportunity for him to convert not just one but two wretches. I couldn't stand the 'praise the lords' that floated through the mobile and cut off the call.

Kocha and I roamed around in the morning, searching for a quiet place. On the way from jail, Kocha had nabbed a motorbike. So thoughtful of him. A vehicle is a must for moving around freely. There was this six-storeyed building that Thampi had constructed out of swindled funds. We found out that there is no one around on its terrace after dark. And then Kontha informed us that he is going to attend a charismatic prayer session. He wants us to accompany him. Great! I told him that we'll meet and finalise it today itself. First I thought of sending Kocha to fetch him. But, no. The asshole might ruin the whole plan by spitting 'dialogues'. So I left him near the building and went to Kontha's place. They were more friendly and again put on a show with Kontha's wife and child as the main cast. 'Take a good look at them,' I felt like telling him. 'Wish them the best, if you want.'

Even as I started the bike, Kontha on the pillion started his holy recital. Why not let him have it, in front of a speeding vehicle, I thought. But there's no point in it. One should be made aware of why one is at the receiving end.

There was some broken furniture on the mossy terrace. We sat on wooden planks around a broken chair. Kontha had already resumed his recital.

'Shaji, let's start with a couple of drinks,' said Kocha.

Kontha looked at us unbelievingly. I noticed terror brewing in his eyes.

'I don't drink anymore,' he mumbled.

'We'll also stop drinking,' I said. 'This will be the last.'

'You have it then. Not me,' he crooned.

What does he think? Not just him, even his dead father and mother couldn't fool me that way. His ploys will not simply work with us.

We caught hold of him and poured into his mouth from the bottle. Fiery rum, that'd make even laggard ponies race. He struggled to break away and spit it out; but a reasonable quantity must've been swallowed. Kocha and I finished off the bottle and threw it away, among the wooden furniture.

'There's no need for you to be so tense,' I advised him. 'We're not going to eat you.'

Kontha looked at us with resentment. 'While you were living like a lord with your woman and child, these two here were counting the prison bars,' Kocha baritoned with the air of an actor. That exactly is his flaw; he cannot resist a dialogue. As if he had a hard time in prison! Just look at him. A fattened pig.

'I'm repenting,' Kontha blurted out in drunken voice. It would've taken a full reel to articulate that word 'repentance' had it been a movie. 'Thampichayan's life should've been given a different direction. The problems between you and him should've been solved,' he continued.

'But we solved him, no?' Kocha threw a bait.

'*Mea culpa, mea culpa, mea maxima culpa*,' Kontha murmured with his hands on his head. He was drunk.

Perhaps we may not have to strain much. He is already floundering like an eel. I tore apart an empty cigarette packet and handed it to him.

'Can he write?' Kocha asked.

I took out a pen and made him hold it. 'Now write,' I said. 'Write as I tell you.'

Kontha looked at us with dead eyes.

'Write,' Kocha barged in with his literary language. 'I repent. I depart. All of this, my sins.'

'My fault,' I changed it into Kontha's language. 'Only my own fault.'

Unsteadily scribbled letters filled the cigarette packet. We had to help him to get it signed. I then folded it and kept it in his shirt pocket.

'Don't stab me,' he pleaded.

'You will commit suicide,' announced Kocha like the hero of a movie, slapping Kontha lightly across his cheeks.

'My family…' Kontha moaned. He was putting up yet another act and I couldn't take it anymore.

'Kocha, you take off that asshole's underwear and stuff it in his mouth,' I shouted. 'We didn't come here to attend a music concert!'

Kontha clutched his mouth in an effort to stop sobbing.

'Except the Lord keep the city…' he looked at us begging for mercy. We lifted him up on to the broken chair. He was quite heavy. 'Fattened on the filthy lucre of Poothalingan Chetty,' I cursed Thampi. We brought the chair to the edge of the terrace. His eyes closed, Kontha was chanting the gospel. It was all silence, except for his prayers and intermittent sobs. Very few vehicles on the road.

Tightly gripping the chair, I tilted it. It took only a small push for the chair to be emptied. After Kontha took flight from the chair, we put it back among the heap.

A feeble thud was heard from down below. I didn't bother to look. No big deal. A job, sort of, that's all.

We climbed down the iron ladder. Kocha was there right behind me. Thought I heard the distant crying of a baby. Aagh … I was fed up. Thought of sitting somewhere all alone, totally free. Kocha started saying something from behind. He must've seen at least a 100 films after he came out on parole. I felt a terrible hatred towards everything.

Holding up the silver-edged knife, I said without looking back: 'Don't you try to show off with the lousy words of bloody hacks. Talk in your words if you've any. One who can't speak with his own tongue, shall not talk anymore.'

~

The Perch

Making a bulls-eye is an art in itself. One has to be very careful. A slight lapse in concentration and the yolk splashes around and one has to be content with the good old double-side fry. Every Sunday morning, I make two bulls-eyes; one for my daughter and one for myself. On Sunday mornings the kitchen is my responsibility, which means that the menu will be very light. Usually it is a loaf of bread and eggs, which I buy on Saturday evenings as I return home. Padmini starts her rounds of the temples early in the morning on Sundays. Perhaps she is skipping breakfast nowadays. I'm not very sure on which days she resorts to this kind of fasting. Whatever it is, she does not like bulls-eye.

She says bulls-eye reminds her of the foetus she was familiar with, in biology texts. I'm not interested in biology. My subject was mathematics and in maths, an egg is compared to an ellipse. Food too had become one of the ingredients for altercations in the monotony of five years of life together. 'In the West they speak of the "seven-year itch", but we have started it a bit early,' we once laughed in the lighter moments after a reconciliation.

'Look, she has wet herself,' I pointed out. After watching for a few silent moments, Padmini, with a detached expression, walked to the kitchen to fetch the mopping rag. I pretended to be deeply immersed in the newspaper, but was observing her all the while.

My seven year-old daughter who was sitting on the floor, her dress soaked in piss, continued playing with strange limb movements.

This child is one of the undeclared contractual obligations of our marriage. It was two years after the death of my daughter's mother that Padmini and I got married. The wedding was the result of a matrimonial ad I had placed in a newspaper. Nothing was concealed; girls or widows with sympathy for a disabled child was the requirement. Padmini was in the fifth year of her widowhood.

We had met for the first time at a friend's place. My daughter wet her clothes on that day too. I was quite taken up by Padmini, who didn't show any hesitation in washing her and changing her dress.

'Why did you opt for a life without children?' I raised this question about her wedded life in which there were no children. Our conversation had been limited to the bare facts. There was nothing romantic about it. Our mindset seemed to be that of people who were about to commit a criminal act.

'At first we did not want a child because of frequent transfers and other preoccupations. And by the time we started thinking about it, his health had deteriorated.'

'What was his problem?' Even though well-briefed by my friend, I pretended curiosity.

'Cancer,' Padmini went on without any show of grief or shock, as if talking about some other life. 'It was a brain tumour.'

'Uma had a severe fever,' I told her about my wife. 'But no one thought a fever would result in death.' In the first few years after her death, my words would break. But, time, I realised, heals broken sentences.

Anu's fingers trembled as she went on knocking the tea mug with a spoon. I had deliberately taken her along with me.

'Anu was a normal child at birth,' I said, taking the spoon from her. 'She too had a fever. But that worsened to an epileptic fit. Nothing has been right since then.'

'Everything will become alright,' Padmini said in an encouraging tone, lifting up the child. She sounded like someone who had undergone a lot. From that day the unwritten contract between us was on; she undertakes the responsibility of Anu. I had been quite apprehensive of bringing up her all alone.

Anu was not a friendly child. She was unable to comprehend or respond to the signs of love and affection. It was the same with her taste buds too. She would eat anything, when hungry. I was the one who had started the Sunday morning habit of bulls-eyes. But I was not sure whether she liked it or not.

It was only some time ago that Padmini indicated her dislike of our food habits. That was the day we had gone to visit the doctor for the first time. The house had remained shut for almost the entire day and we felt the stench of unwashed clothes and stagnant air as we entered.

'What a stench!' Padmini said accusingly, even as she was opening the windows. The visit to the doctor had left her slightly frustrated, I thought.

'Switch on the fan,' I said, laying Anu, who was sleeping on my shoulders, down on to the sofa. Lips slightly parted, she turned to her side in sleep.

'Switching on the fan is not going to make any difference,' her irritation was quite apparent. 'It's the eggs you made in the morning. You may not have cleaned up.'

'We left in a hurry, no? It can be done now.'

'Who is going to do it? Not me! I can't stand the smell of eggs. It's nauseating.'

'So, I'll do all the dishes from today onwards,' I said in a tone of arrogant mockery.

'I didn't mean that,' Padmini lowered her voice. 'I can't wash the dishes you use for making eggs.'

We didn't continue the conversation any further. I stepped into the kitchen and switched on the exhaust fan. A dove, which had established its nest in the hollow of the exhaust, flew away in a hurry. The fan-blades made disconcerting sounds brushing the twigs and dry leaves that were gathered by the dove for strengthening its nest.

Padmini switched off the exhaust fan. 'Let the bird be there,' she said. 'Maybe it wants to lay eggs.'

I was furious. Accuse one that there's a stench and when one tries to get rid of it, prevent it by bringing in something else! Don't these doves have any other nook to perch on and lay eggs?

I took off on my scooter to the town. All the way, I was reviewing the conversation with the doctor and the investigations he had suggested. I was convinced he said enough to suggest that the problem was with Padmini, although he hadn't put it in as many words. After all, I had a child from my first marriage. But at the same time, he had also said that the reports favoured Padmini.

'I don't really see any problems,' said the doctor going through the reports once again. 'Maybe the problem was with her husband,' he added, alluding to Padmini's first marriage.

'He used to take some medicines,' she said with visible enthusiasm.

'It may take some time,' doctor said scribbling something on the case sheet. 'Perhaps we can have some more tests. But luck too has a role, I believe.'

He advised that she should have good sleep and that she should not go out in the sun.

'Will the next child be normal...?' Padmini asked with hesitation.

'Now don't be silly,' the doctor was emphatic. 'First of all, it was not a genetic disorder in her case. And even if it was, the general experience is that such things are not repeated.'

Padmini's visits to temples became more frequent after this. She went to the temples in the locality turn by turn.

The dove became more active in its nest-building activities. The blades of the exhaust fan could hardly turn due to the twigs and strings and leaves. It would only hum when switched on. The black-grey bird was present there almost always.

This soon became another contentious issue.

'What a ruckus you made about the smell of eggs! Now one can't even enter the kitchen because of the stench of pigeon droppings,' I complained.

'It will leave once the eggs are hatched,' she said dismissively.

'That's what I can't understand. Is this the place for laying eggs and hatching?' I fumed.

'No, you will never understand,' she yelled. 'At times, you show less intelligence than even this kid.'

It was like a slap on my face. The child was never brought into any of our altercations. It was another clause of the unwritten contract between us.

My daughter was sitting on the veranda, tearing the pages of a book into shreds. I did not stop her. However, Padmini took the book from the child's hands, gathered the paper pieces and went back into the kitchen. Her face had a paper-like pallor, which revealed neither love nor hate.

The child has not been given a bath as yet. I didn't query Padmini about the delay. But I wouldn't take the initiative too. Let her do it. She had agreed for wedlock fully understanding everything that was involved.

After some time, Padmini came out of the kitchen carrying hot water. Sounds of the tap being turned on and water falling into the bucket came from the bathroom. She then undressed the child, applied oil onto her head and led her to the bathroom.

Anu invariably cries when water is poured on to her head. But today I heard Padmini scolding her. This was rather unusual. Pretending not to have heard anything, I switched on the TV. A polar bear blissfully sleeping in deep snow lit up the screen.

Yesterday I had come earlier than usual from the office and found Anu playing in the courtyard with neighbourhood children. She was soaked in dirt and dust. I could hear sounds from the kitchen. I went inside. White pigeon droppings littered the kitchen floor.

'You ought to show at least as much concern for the child as you show for the dove,' I shouted.

Padmini was taken aback. 'What am I supposed to have done?' she asked with a stunned look.

'Where's Anu?'

'Isn't she playing in the courtyard?'

'Playing! What a shape she is in! Even beggar-children will be cleaner.'

'What are you saying? Is it not me who looks after her? What do you know about the hassles of bringing up such a child?'

'I just mentioned what I happened to see.'

'Is that all? You sounded as if I was neglecting her deliberately. Have I not been cleaning the piss and shit of a child, this grownup? Have I ever discriminated against her? It's all my fate.'

She had started crying.

Crying is one of her weapons. But I was firm. 'Not everyone will understand all these…'

Padmini looked up at me, continuing to weep.

'To understand…' I stopped with the precision of splitting an egg.

'To understand?' she echoed my words with concealed apprehension. I decided not to complete the sentence. It was just the flash of a stroke of lightning. She can as well wait with patience for the thunder.

The dove was cooing from the rectangular receptacle of the exhaust fan. Walking out of the kitchen, I gathered Anu, who was now crying in the courtyard, in my arms. Padmini too had come out.

'Hot water for her bath is ready,' she said. I ignored it totally.

'You are a wretch, with no gratitude,' Padmini broke the unbearable silence that hung about us.

It was for the first time that she was using such words about me. Their obscene violence was scalding…

'You'll not understand, I told you no? Because, you … you are a barren bitch,' I roared.

It was the massive thunder, of the earlier flash of lightning.

Padmini stood still as if electrocuted.

'Barren bitch,' I repeated in booming voice. 'One must know what birth pangs are, to love children.'

I felt I was on the throes of a great victory, as I was washing away the dust and dirt from the body of Anu with lukewarm water.

It being twilight, I didn't pour water on her head. Anu cries only if water is poured on her head.

The sound of Padmini's sobs came from the bedroom. I dressed up the child and went to the town with her on the scooter to buy bread and eggs for the next day's breakfast.

The unlit house seemed to be weeping in loneliness when we returned.

It was me who fed the child that night. Indeed, a difficult task. How much persuasion is required for each gulp…!

I was late getting up on Sunday morning.

Padmini has not gone to the temple as usual. But I didn't bother about her. The floor was littered with pigeon droppings, when I entered the kitchen.

I decided to put an end to this nuisance once and for all, before breakfast.

Bringing a chair, I stood upon it and aimed a blow at the pigeon with a broomstick. It tried to evade the tip, but finally flew out. But then it tried to regain its perch. I struck again. This time it was forced to evacuate the exhaust fan. The dry leaves and the twigs and may be the eggs … I poked them out. I should cover the fan with a mesh from the outside and get rid of this inconvenience for ever, I determined.

Getting down from the chair, I cleared the feathers and the droppings that had fallen on the floor, when I was probing with the broomstick.

Waking up Anu, I tried to brush her teeth. She bit my fingers hard, at least once. But not a whimper from me because I didn't want Padmini to hear, even though it hurt bad…

I sliced the bread, leaving the water to boil for tea.

Now for the customary Sunday morning bulls-eye.

I split the eggs carefully and poured them on to the hot pan. There's invariably a hum that notifies that the fry is ready. Lifting them on to a plate, I sprinkled pepper and salt. Two yellow eyes looking at me? I experienced a strange kind of satisfaction.

After making tea, I brought Anu and seated her on a chair.

She has no idea as to how to have a bulls-eye. I spoon fed her. But the yellow yolk has already been broken.

Anu is not gulping it down; she is playing with it, swirling it in her mouth. I insisted on her swallowing it.

She looked around and spit all that was there in her mouth on to my face. In absolute rage, she also flung the two plates on to the floor.

Losing my control, or whatever was left of it, I slapped her on her cheek. The red hot imprints of three fingers were on her cheek. Shrieking in a high baritone, she rolled around on the floor.

I tried to control my rage. Walking out, I reached for the water tap and washed my face. But the stench would not go away. Eggs have an inevitable stench, it's true.

There were sounds of plates being rearranged from the kitchen. The kid has stopped wailing.

The dove with grey and black feathers was eyeing me from a low branch of the mango tree, just beyond the water tap.

~

The Crying Buddha

If you meet a Buddha on your path, kill the Buddha.

—Zen Master, Linji Yixuan

Winter had just set in when they reached that unfamiliar city. Even the mild chill of early winter was beyond Annie. And so she had put woollen clothes and blankets as the first items on the shopping list. Nandan selected a warm, thick cardigan for Annie and the baby growing in her. He had to manage the setting up of the house—from a nail for hanging the mirror on the wall—to every other tidbit for the household. He ignored the hassles in organising things in view of the impending arrival into their life, which was showing signs of dreariness. He had anyway got used to the climate.

The pregnancy period for Annie was also one of uncertainties. Since their families were not on good terms with them, they had to depend on women's magazines for tips. They had recommended viewing pictures of Farex babies. Nandan cut out pictures from magazines and pasted a few on the wall of their rented house. But the babies shrivelled on the uneven and rough walls. It was the same articles in those women's magazines that had suggested saffron flowers in pure milk for chubby and handsome babies. Both were not easily available in a city. Nandan thought he would seek the help of Ratanlal, the office peon.

On the very next day after Nandan indicated it to Ratan, Yesoda—what an apt name for a milkmaid—came to their residence. Nandan was surprised that, Ratan, perhaps the laziest person in the world, arranged it in such a short time.

He was about to leave for office, when Yesoda came. She had the face of a young girl and the body of an old woman. Strands of her hair were already graying. She stooped a little to talk to Annie. Nandan then found that there was a child on her back, swaddled in old clothes. His feet protruding out of the cloth bundle, hands crossed, head inclined sideways and with wide open eyes, he was almost a fat boy. It was his weight that was making Yesoda stoop.

'The milk should be pure,' Nandan intervened. 'Don't add water to it.'

'God is my witness,' Yesoda swore. 'There is no dishonesty in milk, sir.'

'We've a device that detects if water is added,' Nandan came out with an unadulterated lie.

Yesoda looked at Nandan and Annie with misgivings. She bit her lips and wet them with her tongue, as if gathering courage. 'In that case, you will have to pay three rupees more.'

Annie laughed, but Nadan maintained his serious posture. 'Okay, but we'll stop buying from you the day we find that it is watered milk.'

Yesoda bent down even more and nodded.

'This is a land where even donkey milk is available,' thought Nadan.

'Can't you put that child down?' asked Annie.

'Yes, why should she carry him on her back? He must be at least seven or eight' he thought.

'Inder is retarded,' Yesoda turned and their view of him did too. 'He cannot manage anything on his own.'

'Do you carry him like this throughout?'

'May God save him, Didi! He was late in crying when he was born,' Yesoda said, with a pale smile.

'Can't you put him in one such school?' Annie called after her.

'We had done that for some time. But…' Yesoda turned around and said, as if revealing a secret, 'the first thing he learnt was a horribly filthy word! We thought his not learning to speak was better.'

'Almost a kangaroo,' Nandan attempted a far-fetched comparison, as Yesoda left. Annie was not keen to take it up further and did not respond to his comment. Maybe she is thinking of the baby, which was late in crying. Pregnant women are reluctant to joke about babies, Nandan remembered.

In the morning, when strong wind blew the mist away, they could see Yesoda with her milk pails. She had pulled the pallu of her saree over the head of the boy to shield him from the cold. A brown dog trudged along with them.

'Don't stand outdoors,' Nandan said to Annie.

Annie bent down, looked at her six-month stomach and asked, 'The baby won't feel the cold, no?'

'No, it won't,' Nandan assured her. 'The body must be having some mechanism for it. Anyway, winter will be over soon.' He tied his shoe laces carefully.

'So, we're getting milk now. What about saffron flowers?'

'I'm on the lookout,' Nandan said, starting the scooter. 'I'll get it within a couple of days.'

It was only a month since he was transferred to the city. Except for his office and surroundings, he was not familiar with the city.

Ratanlal was his guide in city matters. Ratanlal had helped him in finding out shops, locating addresses, getting phone and gas connections. Nandan was aware that he was being exploited in return by Ratanlal. He turns up at the office only at 11 in the morning and leaves at four. The way he conducts himself in the office was worse. His mouth was like an oil press that worked nonstop. It was always full of betel leaves and tobacco. The thick red liquid trickling from his mouth stained the chair and created weird maps on the files he carried. The strange thing was no one had any complaints about any of these. What a place! Almost everyone would be having a siesta after lunch, by turns. Maybe it was common knowledge, because visitors too were few in the afternoon.

'Saffron flowers, no?' Ratan asked, spitting out the over-chewed betel leaves through the window. It was four days since Nandan had mentioned it to Ratan. 'Let's enquire at the Chor Bazar,' Ratan suggested with a loaded smile.

Nandan looked at him keenly on hearing about the thieves' market. Ratan smiled, 'That's only a name, sir. I've a few acquaintances there.' He glanced at his old wristwatch, almost as big as a clock. It showed 30 minutes past three. 'Shall we go?' he mimed.

'Later,' Nandan replied in the same sign language.

Nandan carefully weaved the scooter through the crowded street. 'We are going to meet a Pathan,' Ratan said from the pillion. 'A good guy. Knowledgeable too. But keep this in mind…'

'What is it?'

'No bargaining. The Pathan is quite firm about it.'

The Chor Bazar was behind the fort. Roaring business on either side of the narrow street. Vehicles passing through the street sometimes came to a sudden halt due to the heavy crowds. The street-side vendors were calling out loudly to the people passing by. Everything from plastic toys, electronic items and old gramophones to plants, flowers and pets were on sale.

Unending rows of old and new books, bhelpuri stalls, a gypsy with a performing monkey. As if all these were not enough, there was a temple too in the middle. It was very difficult to find one's way through the jostling crowd.

The Pathan with a white turban tied around his head, appeared to be more than six feet tall. His wares were heaped in the small space between two rickshaws. A few jute bags were hanging from his shoulders. He too was calling out to people at the top of his voice. Ratanlal touched his arms. The tall man turned to look at Ratanlal. Obviously the Pathan knew Ratanlal very well.

'Hey, is it you Ratan *bhai*? I thought you too had become a nomad like we people. Okay, tell me, which country were you in, all this while?' he asked in his booming voice. Ratan introduced Nandan to the Pathan. His handshake was so firm, Nandan was afraid the new friendship might cost him his hand.

'Saffron flowers! What bad luck, *bhai*! Just five minutes since the best of the lot was sold off. I'll keep it for you the next time you come. How can I sell low quality stuff to you?'

Nandan regretfully thought that he could have left the office at 3.30.

'Hello Ratansaab,' boomed the Pathan's voice behind them. 'Another lot of significant stuff has come in. I think it could be of interest to this Saab. Would you like to have a quick look at it?'

Nandan was curious. The Pathan handed over charge of his shop to a rickshaw-puller and led them to a staircase landing, squeezing his way through a narrow cleft between two buildings. He then opened a steel trunk and showed them a few stones.

'Stones,' exclaimed Nandan. Stones with a red tinge to them.

'Not plain stones,' the Pathan raised his index finger and said in all seriousness. 'They are precious pieces.'

'What else are these, brother, if not stones?' Ratan asked, opening his betel-tobacco packet, in preparation for a detailed *paan* chewing session.

'Stones, ok,' the Pathan agreed. 'But they are broken boulders.'

'But stones are broken boulders only,' Nandan thought.

'Try to make a guess,' the Pathan said softly.

His guesses did not go beyond stones.

'All of these are the fragments of the Buddha statues.'

'Buddha's statues? From where?' Nandan just could not get it.

There was something exciting in the Pathan's laughter.

'Two Buddha idols that were demolished in Bamian! Brought from across the border. The men at the check-post must have thought that those who carried them were crazy.' He picked up a stone with black edges and continued. 'See, the mark of gunpowder. This is precious sir. Its value is beyond pricing. Keep it in the showcase and you can travel centuries back in time!'

'Will anyone recognise it?'

'Why should anyone recognise it? That it is there, in itself, is a great thing, no?' And you just wait and see, only history will have any market in future. A time will come when even a knife used for killing will fetch crores in auctions. Then you can imagine what the worth of this will be.

Still Nandan was reluctant to buy it.

'You have my word for it. You take it. What a small price to pay, if you consider its real value! And, this statue has a uniqueness.' He patted the stone as if consoling it. 'This was a crying idol. The anguished Buddha.'

On close scrutiny, a slight bulging line, which could be a strand of hair, was visible. The Pathan pointed to it and said, 'This was the head. The weeping eyes were just below it.'

The very idea of a crying Buddha was unbelievable, still Nandan got it wrapped in a jute bag.

'There are only visuals of war these days on the TV,' Annie told Nandan at night. 'While one plane drops bombs, another one drops food packets. I saw pictures of kids running to pick up the packets and switched off the TV.'

'Why?'

'They were just skin and bones. Seeing those kids makes you shudder.'

'Don't watch the news,' Nandan advised her, thinking of the Farex baby pictures the women's magazine had recommended. But how to avoid the newspapers?

He kept the Buddha head on the bedroom window sill and announced: 'It is not mere stone. It is an invaluable Buddha idol.' Annie looked at him with incredulous eyes.

'It was given to me by a Kabuliwala. If we are fortunate enough, he will manage to gather all of the demolished pieces. When put together, it will be a huge statue, even bigger than this house.'

'Anyone can hoodwink you.' There was a hint of anger in her laughter. 'And he says it is a Buddha idol!'

Perhaps thinking of all this, Nandan could hardly sleep. When he finally slept, he started dreaming of mammoth busts. It resembled the scene from a Hollywood movie, which showed huge boulders shaped like human faces. Nandan got up and had a glass of water. He then took the stone and kept it in the drawing room.

In his sleep he thought he heard someone crying.

Yesoda kept her word. The milk she brought was pure and without any water added to it. She was invariably accompanied by the child and the brown dog. Seeing the child, Nandan always had disturbing thoughts about babies who took time to cry out.

Inder made a strange sound upon seeing Nandan's idol. As if responding to Inder's sound, the dog went into a long howl. 'Damn! Should she be asked not to bring the child along?'

'Did you notice? It seems that boy recognised your Buddha,' Annie made fun of him.

Nandan did not respond to her taunt. 'Buddha! Absurd. It is nothing more than a piece of stone.' He should not have fallen for the Pathan's words.

They went to the market again that evening. The Pathan handed over saffron flowers in a pretty little box. Maybe due to the mist and cold, the market was not too crowded. Vehicles plied with headlights on.

'Sir,' the Pathan said, 'I searched and found out another piece that would fit in with the head part of the idol. Please take that too.'

'I'll become a pauper if I start buying everything,' Nandan tried to evade him.

'Take it sir.' He packed the piece in a jute bag and handed it over. Nandan could not disregard the tenor of command in the Pathan's words.

'You will have to close your shop if the Taliban is defeated,' Nandan told him.

'There is nothing like that in business, sir,' The Pathan laughed. 'What guarantee was there that the Americans would not have demolished the Bamian rocks.'

'America would never have done such a thing,' Nandan was emphatic.

'It is not correct. It is circumstances that turn rocks to dust, sir. Say, Osama had taken refuge behind the statues. What would have happened then?'

Nandan grinned at the Pathan's logic.

'Let the war be over, *bhai*,' Ratan said. 'Then you can return.'

'I've not decided yet. The Afghans are big fools at times. It has reached such a state that anyone can go and start a war there. Just show them a Hindi movie and they will forget everything else. Anything will get acceptance there for at least a period of time. Do you want to hear the story of how a Pakistani youth came and taught us communism?' He paused and then continued, 'He studied in London and then came to our mountains. He organised the shepherds. The struggle was against the Pakistani army.'

The Pathan elaborated, 'The Pakistani commanders did not fire a single shot at the shepherds. Instead they killed the entire herd of sheep. The people did not have any other livelihood. Nothing to eat. They too started dying. The conflict was over. The youth returned to London to study what went wrong.'

Shifting the jute bags to his other arm, the Pathan smiled sadly. 'We Afghans are a community that cried late at birth. Mere dullards. We take more time even to crawl on our knees.'

Even a community that delays in crying out has a problem. Nandan suddenly remembered Yesoda's child.

A terrified Annie had shut herself in, when Nandan reached home with the saffron flowers.

'Please, don't take it as a joke.'

'You tell me what it is.'

'That idol is moaning.'

Nandan looked at her and tried to smile. But Annie was not smiling. He was upset.

'I was in the kitchen doing dishes in the afternoon. It was then that I heard. I came out to see who it was. But there was no one. Maybe it was a false sensation, I thought. But then I heard it again. From there,' she pointed her finger. Nandan could see alarm in her eyes.

Nandan took out the stone from the bag and placed it alongside the earlier one. The new piece fitted in very well with the old! As if it was cut out after drawing a line. The Pathan's words barged into his mind, 'it was just below the head,' the crying eyes of Buddha.

He too then heard a moaning sound. But it was all silence after that.

Nandan gathered the pieces of the statue and dumped it in a corner, where things to be disposed of were heaped. He covered the stones with some old vessels.

'Buddha has been got rid of,' Nandan informed Annie. But she didn't seem to register it.

The next day Nandan had to go to the railway station to receive his aunt and her husband, who were coming to assist them. The ill feelings that were created in the family due to Nandan's wedding to Annie had not died down. His aunt was the only one willing to be with them in their time of need.

'That Pathan was here, sir,' Ratan told him when he reached the office at noon.

'What made him come?'

'He got the idol's eye. It is quite big.'

'We've no need of them, Ratan.'

'He is quoting a very low price, sir,' Ratan tempted him.

'I don't want it. There is no space in the house.'

Annie got angry with him that night. 'Got rid of it! You lied to me, no? I found it out. It cried again.'

'Aunty heard it?'

'I did not tell her. She too would've heard, had she listened.'

He drove some distance on his scooter carrying the jute bag and then threw it away. That night he slept as if senseless, in some strange sense of security.

'That stupid statue should not have been brought here. My thoughts start straying even when I see the baby pictures,' Annie told him, while they were waiting for Yesoda in the morning.

'Don't bother about anything,' Nandan tried to distract her by talking about their home town.

And then Yesoda walked in with that jute bag.

'Why did you bring it?' Nandan shouted at her. Inder was not with her.

'The dog was barking at it, Didi,' Yesoda said. There is some hoodoo in this. Yesterday Inder was frightened seeing this. That's why he did not come with me.'

Nandan picked up the stones and took it along with him to the office. This has to be returned to the Pathan, even if he does not refund the money.

'But he has already left,' Ratan smiled. 'The war in his country is almost over.'

'Then what happens to these stones?'

'What about them? I feel the Pathan lied about them. If you don't want them, let them remain outside the office. Maybe they will become useful when the rains come.'

'Buddha as stepping stones?'

'What use could be there for the Buddha who lets himself be demolished?' Ratan spat the betel leaves he was chewing through the window.

Annie told him that day that she felt she heard someone sobbing in the distance. It sounded as painful as someone bidding goodbye.

Will there be a delay in his baby crying out? This thought seized Nandan all of a sudden.

He felt a child overgrown beyond its age, gesticulating instead of speaking, straddling his shoulders like a ghoul. He was trembling. Nandan did not want Annie to notice the change in his mood and he started tinkering with the remote, changing channels. Surfing through wars and terror attacks, he settled down at a cartoon channel.

'This is the channel most suitable for us,' he told Annie in all seriousness. A fat bunny grinned at him from the screen.

And then the sobs left them alone.

After few days, when Nandan was in his office, Annie gave birth to a baby girl, two weeks ahead of her due date. It was a clear day with little mist and he reached the hospital on his scooter. His aunt who was waiting in front of the labour room told him, 'Caesarian could not be avoided. The baby is slightly underweight.'

He walked through the long corridors of the big hospital, climbed the stairs and reached the doctor's room on the second floor. The doctor, who was jotting down something, smiled at him.

'Her weight is below normal. But it does not matter,' she said. 'There seems to be something wrong with the calculation of the date.'

'Did she cry, madam?'

'Cry? Why?' She looked at him with astonishment.

'The baby. Didn't the baby cry?'

The doctor thought for a while and then said: 'O, yes. There was an immediate cry. Everything was okay.'

Nandan felt a weight sliding off his back.

While climbing down the staircase, he heard baby cries from many rooms. It was like a musical programme with different levels. 'After a long time, it is now that I'm not terrified of cries,' Nandan thought.

~

Three Fingers

When I stepped into the office after two days' leave, our boss sent for me in his cabin and handed over a letter to me.

'This is for you. Your friend, Mr Joseph had come to meet you yesterday.'

'Joseph?' Before I could ask 'Which Joseph?' he smiled in an unusually friendly manner and gestured at me to occupy a chair.

'So you are a writer, eh?' he even seemed to get up from his chair as he said this.

A friend by name Joseph, a letter entrusted by him, and the question, 'You are a writer, eh?' To put it briefly, I was not able to make out anything. It was true that I had published a mostly unnoticed novel few years ago, but I did not have any pretensions to be a writer. I maintained silence, as I was not sure how to answer his question.

'All such activities ceased after I got into a job and family.' I did not respond to it as it was an oft-heard sentiment. How did this man come to know of my literary efforts, which even I had forgotten?

'Not knowing anything about our colleagues is our own failure. See, I came to know of this only yesterday. When your friend showed me the book. I would not have believed it, had your photo not been there on the cover.'

I tried to open the letter.

'Don't you remember?' he asked, 'A friend called Joseph? Slightly old guy. It has been some time since you met, he said.'

'Joseph? I just don't get him.' I looked at my boss in silence.

'Your friend is a peculiar character, you know. An interesting fellow. He had all of us in eating from his palm in just half an hour.'

Who is this guy, this my friend with the magic wand smart enough to tantalise almost 20 middle-aged people … I had absolutely no idea.

'I don't remember having a friend with the name Joseph.'

'Eh, no. it cannot be. He knows you well. Did he not bring the novel with your picture? Eh, what's the name of that book?'

'*Mirage*,' I mumbled awkwardly.

'Yes, that's it. It is a very good title. If I were to write a novel, I too would have named it in a similar manner.' He stopped talking as the phone started ringing, but continued as the rings stopped. 'There is no chance of you forgetting him. He is a tremendous artist. He can draw anyone's picture within no time. Doesn't even take five minutes. Wonderful.'

As if to prove it, he opened the drawer of his table and displayed his own picture. I could see our boss with his large ears and chubby nose coming alive from that picture completed in just four or five strokes.

Just one look at the sketch and for me it was like someone wiping away the last 10 to 12 years. Like rivers that had ceased to flow at some point of time in the past, finding a source again and starting to flow. Memories like new sprouts on the dried wild tree in the forest. I was drenched in the rain of memories.

Monayi. Very few used to know him by his full name, Joseph Monayi.

And then I heard the rattling of an old typewriter. Also the noises of getting on to the third floor of a crumbling building.

Dark evenings in a distant town, advertisement boards, dusty days, men, huge bullocks with raised heads walking crammed between auto rickshaws and buses, streets which would turn into mud pools even after a short shower.

I was there for three years from 1990 to '93. At least a few may recollect an old three-storey building that was visible from the traffic island where the museum road ended and in which a Sindhi finance company was functioning. I had an occasion to visit that place recently. That building has been demolished and a new skyscraper occupies the place. Drastic changes.

'Dayal Investments'—it used to function in a small room. The small name board hung on the door was the only evidence of the company's existence there. Though the office room was small and the facilities were limited, the number of people who had deposited their money there was huge. However, this was not publicised. Merchants, especially merchants who were not Malayalees invested there and also availed credit facilities. They also bid chits and invested in bonds, which would mature within five years and yet pay back double the investment.

I used to work there during that period. In fact I came to that place only because of that job. The ambition of becoming a writer and the experience of working as a proof reader in an evening daily at a very low salary were the only qualifications I had. But here, I was the one who looked after the accounting in Dayal Investments. Accounting means not just accounting. My routine there started off with cutting open incoming letters, going to the bank and meeting the shopkeepers in person to dispatching numerous certificates, drafts, receipts etc., to Bombay. Affixing stamps, putting letters in envelopes and posting them was also my duty. The scheduled job time was eight to eight. But often I had to work late. Around nine in the morning a typist would come to help me out. He used to leave by six. The typist was on a temporary posting and he was paid daily wages. Because of it the roll over of the typists was high. During my time at least four or five typists followed one after the other. Hundreds of certificates had to be typed out everyday. There were stringent conditions like no errors in name, date or the amount. The salary paid to them was a pittance. There would be deductions from that amount for every mistake committed. The company was quite strict about it and I couldn't do anything even if I wanted to. Computers were just becoming popular.

I got fed up with that job in a matter of few months. There was hardly time for anything else after office. Let alone writing, even the books I had brought with me for reading, were gathering dust. I had no time even for looking around for another job. Sometimes even food had to be skipped. I was in a contract with the company for three years. They had got the bond signed by me on stamped paper. Abandoning the job before the stipulated term meant reimbursing 10 times the monthly salary. Moreover, getting another job would have been very difficult. And if at all I was getting one, I was apprehensive that it would pay less. They were indeed paying me slightly more than the average salary paid by private firms. And moreover I was in charge of the office, at least apparently.

Monayi was the third typist after my entry into the company. He worked for about three months with me. He was the one who worked for the least period as a typist at that office. When a typist quit, which the company hardly noticed, a small ad was placed in the Classifieds. Something like 'A reputed financial company needs an experienced typist' or so. At least 20 aspirants would appear. It was not a very difficult task to select an apparently harmless fellow from them. This time, however, a guy came enquiring before the ad was out, perhaps on hearsay.

It was noon. I had gone out for lunch and when I returned, there was this man standing in front of the closed office door.

'Joseph Monayi,' he made a self-introduction. I came seeking a job, he said and also mentioned that he knew typing.

He looked much more aged than the average employment seeker and was clad in a *mundu* and long kurta. Graying hair was allowed to grow long and was neatly combed on either side of his ears. He was wearing spectacles and his hands were tucked away in the pockets of the kurta.

'We can give it a try if you are good at typing,' I said. Somehow I had the feeling that he would not be up to it.

Since the typist was not available during that week, there was a lot of work pending.

He repeated that he knew typing. 'I type with the index fingers. But I can finish all the pending work in time,' he said.

I handed over certain documents to him, not quite convinced.

I was watching him removing the plastic cover of the typewriter and feeding a stack of paper into it.

When he started typing I was shocked to notice that three fingers were missing from his left palm. He was typing using only the index fingers of both hands. The three fingers looked as if they were cut. The ends were stunted. I could not bear looking at them. We two did not talk about it.

But listening to the rhythm of the typewriter I understood that Monayi had very good speed. He was typing without making any kind of errors. Corrections were not needed. I didn't have to supervise his work.

He became familiar with all his duties in the office within a week. He even started assisting me in my tasks in his spare time.

'It is a good thing that you joined this company,' I told him. 'Otherwise I couldn't leave this office even by eight.'

Monayi turned towards me and smiled. He had finished his work and was standing at the window gazing the horizon.

Now that I was getting some spare time, I made final drafts of a few stories and sent them to different magazines. All of them came back promptly.

Monayi would leave the office at noon. He went home for lunch. He did not have the practice of bringing a lunch packet with him. He had told me he did not live nearby. Often he would be late coming back after lunch. During some of those days Monayi would not work in the afternoon. He would sit hunched or will make a *paan-beda* with all elaborations. In what seems to others as an unending ceremony, he would've chewed and spat out any number of betel leaves. One followed by another. Even the habit of chewing *paan* was quite strange in his case. It was not a matter of routine for him. Sometimes he would suddenly stop working and go out. He would return only after considerable time. Sometimes he would come running by the closing hour, all in a sweat. I did not make that an issue as the tasks assigned to him were being done with promptness. Maybe because of the big age difference, private discussions were very rare between us.

One afternoon, Monayi asked me, 'Do you believe in astrology?'

I was baffled for a moment because that question came from nowhere, so out of context.

'Just a question, that's all,' Monayi tried to elaborate. These are times when people have faith in everything. Astrology, palmistry … anything. You can't walk around without running into believers.'

'Any specific reason for you to feel so, now?'

'There's something interesting,' he said looking at me with friendly eyes. Then he got up from the typewriter and came to the window. He pointed at something on the ground below.

'Come and take a look. Just as I said these are the times when people bestow faith in anything. Just look at the crowd.'

I got up without much interest. There was a crowd on the street. It was rather unusual. Underneath a shady tree, there was a saffron-clad palmist, a woman. But that was not a surprise; I've been seeing her from the time I first came here. The waiting shed in front of the bus stand was her usual place.

'Isn't she the palmist?' I asked.

'Do you know her?' he seemed surprised.

'Of course. I've had my palm read by her.'

'You have faith in all these?' Monayi repeated his first question. 'How do my beliefs assume importance,' I thought.

'Oh, it was only for fun sake,' I tried to evade the question.

'What all did she predict?' there was excitement in Monayi's voice.

'It was quite some time ago. Nothing much. Just two or three things,' I said. 'One was that I would go away from this town.'

'That would surely happen when your contract expires. Moreover, being young it is easy to guess that you will get another job,' Monayi argued.

'She said that I will join another job in another town.'

'Naturally'.

'She also predicted that this company will shut down.'

Monayi looked at me rather unconvinced. He did not comment on it. It required extraordinary guts to announce that this North Indian company, which had a good name among its clientele and a solid history of 50 years, would shut down. I too had been surprised hearing this particular prediction.

'When was all this said?' Monayi asked wiping his specs.

'Quite some time back. Perhaps during my early days here.

'I don't believe in all this,' Monayi said. I've been on a campaign against all these for quite some time. I was an activist of the rationalist movement. I've assisted in their publishing efforts. I've been a participant of every protest and agitation against meditation centres and prayer conventions. I was among those who protested against *makarajyothi* at Sabarimala by lighting a big fireball. That was a time…'

I returned to my chair and resumed my work. The clattering of the typewriter also resumed after sometime.

'But is there anyone who is not interested in one's future?' He continued as if in continuation of where we had left off. He was talking in a very low voice as if conveying a secret. 'If she is ready to read my palm I too would go to her. Whether I believe it or not, I would listen to it.'

'What do you mean by if she is ready?' I almost laughed out. 'You just have to go to her. For her it is only a question of earning money.'

'I've some hesitation in extending my hand to her in front of all those people. I opposed all these once, no? Even now it is only a curiosity; nothing to do with belief.'

'It doesn't matter. You should have your palm read. I'll come with you. We'll leave the office a bit early in the evening. There will not be much of a rush by that time.' I tried to back him up.

'It seems she does not read all the palms. She has a specific number at which she stops. She has some sort of divine powers, someone in the crowd was saying,' Monayi laughed in derision.

'Divine power! I don't know.' I continued working. 'But I know one thing: she doesn't have eyesight.'

Monayi suddenly stopped typing and gaped at me in disbelief.

'Yes. That is it. She reads palms using a twig or by touching with fingers,' I said.

'Come on! That would only be acting!'

'That's what I too had thought. But…' I continued lowering my voice. 'I've got proof for that. One day I happened to see her squatting and urinating in a public place. It was somewhat dark. Men will do it. But no woman would do it if there is even a remote chance of anyone seeing it. However old she may be. Right? She did so believing that there is no one around. In fact there were a few people waiting for the last bus.'

That evening, we got off from the office slightly early and saw the old lady all alone under the tree. The fancy of the people must have subsided. Monayi walked up to the palmist, after making sure none of his acquaintances were there, frantically looking around. I was quite sure that there was no one who knew Monayi in that town. No one had ever come to the office asking for him. Nor did he get any phone calls. His home was somewhere in the south, he had mentioned. He had made a living by doing small jobs like this one and by teaching in tutorial colleges. I had never bothered to find out the veracity of these bits of information.

She was clad in a loose yellow dress. A three-fold *rudraksha mala* was looped around her neck. She did not have any other ornaments. She seemed to be lost in meditation when we approached her.

She took Monayi's extended palm in her hand. I then recalled how I had an unusually cold sensation when I had touched her. It was like touching the hand of a dead person. She took a twig and traced the lines on Monayi's palm. Then she kneaded his fingers very slowly. Monayi had sat down tucking his left hand from which fingers were missing, on his lap.

'You shifted from the bus stand to here, eh?' I tried some small talk with her.

'Dust storms have become very common there.' She nodded and smiled at me. There were very few teeth in her mouth. Whatever was left there were decaying or had heavy *paan* stains.

'Your fingers are unusually long,' she said slowly. That was true. It was then that I noticed, Monayi's fingers were very long.

'You are an artist,' She continued slowly, shaking her dangling ears that had long pouches. Monayi stared at her without making any attempt to respond to her. Perhaps she did not expect any response at all and hence she continued to dab at the lines on his palm with her twig.

'But you did odd jobs to survive. You have been an accountant; you've worked as a document writer and record keeper. You also must have taught children. All this because you had some problems in continuing as an artist.' She stopped moving the twig. 'And later on someone has blocked you from continuing with it.' Then she resumed the movement of the twig. The twig was moving like an animate being, I felt.

Monayi did not respond to anything. We were sitting by her side, slightly bent forward. The long break the old woman took between her observations made me restless. During the time it took for a word to form at the tip of her tongue like a big drop of rain and fall on the ground, she soothed her own palm with the twig or massaged its tip as if sharpening it. I found it strange that she kept her eyes closed all the while.

The old woman pressed Monayi's palm with her own and then smelled it. She repeated this action couple of times. Suddenly she dropped the palm as if shocked. She picked up her twig and placed it in her satchel.

'What happened?' Monayi opened his mouth for the first time. I could recognise the anxiety in his question.

'Nothing. That is all,' the hag said. Her eyelids opened. I noticed the fickle movements of her dull eyeballs like the sun extinguished by the white ocean.

As she continued to remain silent, we stood up. I felt that her hands were trembling when she accepted money from Monayi.

The streetlights were on. We walked on the edges of the headlight beams of the speeding vehicles. I posted the envelopes that I had brought with me, in a roadside postbox. Then we got some roasted groundnuts from a tricycle vendor and stood there munching.

'You please carry on. I'll get a bus,' Monayi said. 'See you tomorrow.'

'So, you now believe in palmistry?' I asked him before parting.

'But what great things did she reveal?' Monayi put the question back to me with a smile.

The next day Monayi was absent for the first time since he joined the company. He called in the evening and reported sick. He was having a severe headache since the morning. It used to recur occasionally. But he had been free of it for a long time. He was taking medicines and hoped to be better by the next day. He finished the call confirming that he would be at the office tomorrow.

The day that followed turned out to be an important one for me. That was the day on which a short story written by me was published for the first time, that too in a fairly popular weekly. Like any other beginner, I too had the feeling of having attained something worthy. Now that the prime barrier has been crossed, I was confident that I would be able to survive in the field. I bought a copy of the weekly and leafed through it several times. I was trying to guess the manner in which a reader would reach the pages on which my story was printed. One may leaf through the pages from the front while another may do it from the last page. I also imagined those readers who might take a look at the contents, notice my name and go straight to the concerned page. Needless to say, every time I picked up the weekly, my reading was confined to my story alone.

I didn't have any friends nearby for celebrating the occasion. So I remained in the office bound by the business of the company, but extremely pleased with myself. All the while

Monayi was typing furiously. I thought maybe he is typing the previous day's certificates too.

During the lunch recess I was preparing to dispatch the certificates he had typed out. I copied the first address into a notebook. That was the record of our outward mail. 'Joseph Monayi, 303, Kallar Lane'. I felt a slight familiarity with that address.

I took up the next one. Eh, the same address ... I was baffled. I scanned the lot Monayi had typed. I was stunned. Monayi had typed out only one name and one address in all the certificates. His own name and address. Joseph Monayi, age 46. I was wondering what had gone wrong with this guy, who had never made a single error till then.

I picked up the lot when Monayi returned to his seat. He was sweating and trembling. His face had become red hot.

'What happened Monayi?' I kept the stack of certificates aside. 'You are sweating profusely.'

'Nothing, absolutely nothing. A severe headache is not leaving me alone.'

'You didn't take any medicine?'

He did not reply and sat with his head bent over the table. I decided not to disturb him for a while.

'She, that palmist...' Monayi turned towards me and said.

'That old woman? Why, what happened to her?'

'Eh, nothing as such. But she is hiding something from me,' Monayi's voice was trembling. 'I was standing by her side all of yesterday, waiting for the crowd to go away. She was surrounded by people practically the whole day.'

So Monayi had availed a day's leave for talking to the old woman? What is wrong with him? I thought of the general saying that extreme atheists end up as sanyasins. I did not feel that there was any substance in what she had told him about his past and future. Palmists and astrologers are like that. They will make artists of everyone. They will vaguely suggest that there are obstructions in the path. Which astrologer will deny the existence of an enemy? That was what I had felt when I had heard her telling him about someone obstructing him. I was of the view that all these are to be treated as just fun.

'Finally I got her for myself just a little while ago. I showed her my hand, without telling her that she had read it once.'

'And then?'

'She broke into abuses as soon as she touched my palm. 'Pig, you pig' she shouted. 'You had come to me day before yesterday, no? You thought I forgot? Get lost with your stinking hand.'

I was aghast. 'Monayi, what is it on your hands? She had smelled it the other day too.'

'That's what I don't understand. She hounded me away. I felt very bad. You know that there is nothing wrong with my right hand.' He raised the long and slender right hand of his, as if to make sure. 'Even then I had washed it thoroughly before I went to her. But still she disgraced me. When she started shouting and howling, the nearby shop keepers and auto drivers rushed at me.'

He was totally shattered, I noticed. I felt it was not the opportune moment to take up the wrongly typed certificates and so I kept the bundle aside.

'Let it pass,' I said to change the subject. 'Today is a good day for me.'

Monayi looked at me dispassionately. His thoughts are full of that palmist and the crowd that surrounded him following the dressing down by her.

I handed over the weekly which had carried my story, 'Here, my story is published in this magazine.'

Monayi was on his feet as if he had heard something very strange. He felt the pages of the weekly with his fingers and gazed at the illustrations of the characters. I could see his face brightening with delight.

'So you are a writer, eh? And I was not aware of it despite sitting and working together all these days.'

'Nothing big about it no? Moreover, this is my first published story,' I was all humility.

He finished reading the story in a matter of minutes. Then he shook hands and said: 'It's good. But when did you write this?'

'Much earlier,' I said. 'Just that I brushed it up after coming here.'

'You should continue writing,' Monayi said in an encouraging tone. 'You should publish a collection of stories.'

The erroneously typed bundle of certificates slipped from my mind till the office closed. But I told him about it when locking up.

'My attention wavers at times. Then what happens is I continue repeating whatever I was doing. I won't even be aware of what I am doing,' Monayi accepted without any hesitation. 'What had gone wrong? Are there too many errors? I'll retype them tomorrow. Please pardon me this time. It was not intentional.'

'It's ok.' I felt a fondness towards him for having admitted his guilt.

There were a few future seekers in front of the palmist even at that time. We ignored her.

'Shall we have a cup of tea?' I asked.

'Tea? Will it suffice? Especially on the day you have turned a writer?' Monayi laughed and continued, 'My headache is still troubling me. By the by, do you drink?'

'I've had a beer once,' I said.

'Then let's go to a bar,' he said. 'But I don't drink beer.'

There was a small bar at the end of the street and we selected the least crowded corner. He ordered a cheap brand of rum I noticed. Rum is the drink of frequent drinkers I had heard. The lower caste among alcohol.

'I'm drinking after almost two years,' he said.

'That's interesting,' I took a gulp of the beer and added, 'anyway drinking regularly is not advisable.'

'True. My doctor has advised me against drinking.' He seemed to be reluctant to continue.

'But what exactly is your ailment?' I asked, 'do you have any heart problem?'

Monayi just smiled instead of answering me. Alcohol seemed to have cheered him up.

'I was thinking,' Monayi finished his drink and kept the glass on the table with a slight bang. 'What's it that the palmist lady is trying to withhold from me?' he then went on to smell his right palm.

'But I can guess,' he said very slowly. 'Sometimes I myself smell my palms. Just like anyone else. And every time I used to get that smell.'

'What kind of smell?' I asked him with curiosity.

'Blood.' He whispered as if revealing a secret.

I could only look at him intently in silence.

'But I was not shocked. The scent of blood was familiar to me.' He stopped speaking for a moment and extended his left palm towards me. 'This still reeks of foul blood, no?'

I had raised my beer mug for a sip, but I put it back on the table.

'But you know that I did not show this hand of mine to her.'

'Palmists normally read the right hand of men.'

He withdrew his extended left hand and stared at me. He rubbed his palms vigorously. In the mystifying red light of the bar, the vacancy left by the missing fingers of his left hand disturbed me.

'What happened to these fingers?' I asked him. So far I had been reluctant to ask him about it.

'These?' He raised his left hand which had only two fingers and continued in a very light air, 'Nothing as such. I cut them off.'

Words seemed to have been cut off from me.

I felt that blood was still oozing from the wounds of the cut-off fingers.

He did not bother about my silence. He poured some water into his glass and had a mouthful, all the while staring steadily into my eyes.

'It required a broad chisel,' he said holding the fingers of his right hand close together as if indicating the dimensions of the chisel.

I raised the beer mug again. I felt it had gone too bitter as the glass touched my lips.

'Certain limbs are a burden for man.' He ordered one more peg and said to me, 'Especially for an artist. They tend to divert your attention.'

Artist. That was the word the palmist had used. He seemed to be reading my mind.

'Once I used to do wood sculpturing. I made use of one of those chisels,' Monayi said as if explaining.

I did not respond. I was afraid to look into his eyes.

'You are right, my friend. That old woman has insight. I am unable to find any other logic. What she said was correct; I used to paint a lot.'

'You don't paint these days?'

'Yes, I do. But only in the mind. He smiled sadly. 'Doctor has asked me not to draw on paper.'

I noticed his abrupt ending of conversation when the word 'doctor' came up.

'Once I start I may not stop. It is a syndrome. Sometimes I continue to draw the same picture again and again.'

'Like the certificates in the morning, no?'

He nodded accepting my words.

'That old hag is a witch,' he said sipping from his next glass. 'She knows everything, everything.'

'Monayi, what is your problem in making pictures? Don't you remember her reference to it?'

'She was quite right,' he agreed. 'I've been prevented. Everyone knows that I will go on drawing and painting otherwise. That old witch can read my entire life span like a book.'

'Why are you being prevented?' I repeated my question.

'It is not as if anyone stopped me from it. But there were prohibitive circumstances.' He continued in a low tone, 'Where do you get paint and brush and canvas in a mental asylum?'

He continued to drink, while I had stopped with one bottle of beer. However, Monayi seemed to have lost all sense of time and went on drinking without any limit.

Most of the tables had become vacant. Bearers were impatiently waiting in the wings for us to finish.

Suddenly he stood up and with great agitation caught hold of both ends of my shirt collar and shook me up.

'An author! You Pomeranian puppy, what is that great literature you and the kind of you produce? What insight on life do you guys have for writing? Leftovers of someone else's creations? Or is it the graphic description of sexual encounters you have managed to watch on the sly?'

I tried to loosen his hands when the tips of the cutoff fingers touched my hands.

'A generation of transgenders without any experience of life.' He freed his hands and collapsed on the chair.

I called for the bill.

Monayi was rocking to and fro while getting down the steps of the bar. I held him close to me but he was slipping like a fish unable to maintain balance.

'Forgive me,' he said after we got out. 'I blabbered lot of nonsense. Please do not take it seriously. Forgive me!'

'Doesn't matter,' I said. 'Where do you live?'

He fished out a purse from his pocket and took out a soiled visiting card from it.

The address on it was of a distant town. It must have been his earlier residence, I guessed.

'This is an old card.' I gave it back to him.

'Oh, did I give you the old card? Sorry, I don't have a card with the present address.' He slumped on the last step of the bar.

'I know your address,' I said, recalling the wrongly typed certificates, 'It's 303 Kallar Lane, isn't it?

Monayi gave me a strange look. He seemed to be surprised that I had taken note of his address.

The place was not very far off; but even the last bus in that direction had left some time ago.

I stopped an auto rickshaw and somehow or other pushed Monayi inside. As the rickshaw left the yellow street lights behind and sped through a deserted road, the events of the day paraded in my mind, as if in a movie. Were all those my delusions? Maybe no such things had happened. My story couldn't have been published. Monayi, who never makes even a single error, could not have typed his own name in all the certificates. And we have not gone into a bar—I attempted another screenplay.

Monayi's trembling body was brushing against mine intermittently. He was looking out into the dark.

There was no change in his mood even when we reached Kallar Lane. It was only when the auto driver asked us to get down that I understood we had arrived.

I stood there for a while, not knowing which direction to take. There was no one around. When my eyes became familiar with the darkness and the dim light of the street lamp, I could make out couple of paths and house numbers. I stumbled along a narrow path that had a board saying 303, holding on to Monayi who was stumbling all the way.

The path was so narrow that two persons could barely walk side by side. We passed a few shop-like structures with wooden planks for walls. There was no light at all. Two dogs lying about on the street casually glanced at us and merely shifted their position without making any sounds.

After covering some more distance, I became apprehensive that we were not on the right track. Monayi was still maintaining a stony silence. But after a few more steps I spotted a dim light streaking out through the wooden planks of a room. I stopped.

Monayi looked at me intently. The light reflected from his tired eyes.

He slipped out of my hold and started banging at the wooden planks of the room. He sat down on the ground after knocking three or four times. I understood that we have indeed arrived at the correct place.

But the eerie silence continued. No one seemed to have heard the knocks.

'There is someone else inside,' Monayi told me in a low voice. 'That's why there is a delay in opening the door.' He seemed to sharpen his ears.

'See, see, painting has been stopped. Now the colours and brushes are being packed up. That sound is the rustling of clothes,' he was whispering like the chanting of a mantra.

I could not make out what he was saying. I saw the door being opened after a while.

The day's wonders were not yet over, it seemed. The woman who opened the door looked like an angel. I felt my eye lids closing due to the light emanating from her eyes. I had never seen someone that beautiful. Her beauty was beyond words. There was some sort of impropriety in such a woman living with a rough and fossil-like Monayi, I felt. She could not be called a woman. She was really a girl. The pale sari she had draped was not suitable for her. She was not wearing any ornaments other than two small ear studs. Her bare neck reminded one of swans. An inexplicable kind of jealousy got ignited and started burning in my mind.

Monayi did not speak to her. He went straight away into the small rooms as if in a search or investigation. His lean body was swaying from side to side.

'I'm a colleague of Monayi,' I said apologetically to the angel.

'Ichayan is drunk, no?' she asked sobbing. 'Doctor had ordered no to drinks.'

'I was not aware of it,' my head bowed down. It was a relief to get out of the range of her aura.

'The back door is open,' Monayi who had just returned from his inspection said in a trembling voice. 'There are signs of trickling paint. They escaped. I was late by a moment.'

He was trembling nonstop.

'Saved him, no?' His voice was full of vengeance. He then pulled the end of her sari and examined it.

The girl covered her face with her hands and started out crying.

'Who were you searching for, Monayi?' I asked. He responded with a mocking smile.

'You do not know anything. I had told you no, that your writing does not have the backing of experience. So I will call it trash.'

I did not feel insulted. The excitement of the publication of my story had drained from me by then.

He continued to walk around still in search. He watched her crying with disdain.

'You are crying!' he exclaimed. 'Very good acting.'

As I turned to get away from there, he stopped me with the finger-cut left hand.

'Are you leaving litterateur? You can easily write a novel about me. I am material for a novel … hahaha,' he laughed uproariously.

'But I'm a bad artist. My story also will be bad.' He picked up a pencil, looked at me and started sketching.

He extended the sketched paper to me. It was a sketch of mine. I was astonished. He had sketched me quite accurately with just a few lines and that too within very little time.

'You know her, no?' He asked me all of a sudden. I did not know how to respond. How was I to know a girl whom I was meeting for the first time? He had already started drawing on another paper.

'You knew this address and also this room. How accurately you brought me here!' He laughed with vengeance. 'Even the dogs in this lane are familiar with you. They did not even bark. Che … what a fool I am!'

I was shocked. I cursed the moment I stepped into the bar with him.

'Don't worry. Many people come here to be with her. I have not been surprised by that. But when I get into a bus and reach here at noon, those guys would disappear.'

I was greatly upset. I should not have come here at this time of night with him.

'You and the like of you will think that those guys come here with desire for her. Fools! That is the problem with writers.

Peeping into bedrooms! No real life experience…' a ridiculing laughter followed. 'But the truth is not that. Guys, renowned artists, they come here. For drawing her picture. I know that. Because I too was an artist once.'

In the dim light of the room, the girl crying with her palms covering her face was like a magical statue. It was a mystery how she happened to be living with this man.

'None of them could complete it. I would somehow reach here before that. If anyone succeeded in capturing her on the canvas, do you know, the greatest painting in the world would happen. A beautiful nude *yakshi.* As for me, I destroyed them. All of them.' He continued to whisper.

He was now sketching his own picture. He tore it into pieces in a sudden fit of rage.

'People tore me up like this,' he shouted violently shaking his hands. 'Drawing nude is a matter concerning the artist only. No doctor, no pig has any right to prevent it.'

I had an urge to run away from Monayi. However, a mean and despicable instinct to listen to the unusual unfolding of an obscene story grew in me at the same time.

'She in her life was an old picture torn into pieces by many,' he said. 'At last, I recovered her by meticulously pasting the shreds.'

'But not out of human kindness, mind you,' he laughed out loud. 'No artist will have any sympathy for anybody, except for himself. I took up her responsibility only for the sake of painting her.'

'I've spent weeks together painting her. Searching for a perfect nude. She sat in front of me in the nude for days and nights. To sleep with her was never my objective. Painting her was my aim. Because there were many who had slept with her. But I alone could paint her at that time. This was at a time when at least a hundred would be ready to pose for just a hundred rupees. I myself have painted so many of them! Like trash! But I went awry when I painted her. But I persisted. I strongly believed that by correcting and touching I would reach perfection. However an intolerable sense of failure had seized me. I punished myself for my follies. Like this.' He raised his left hand with the cut fingers. He thrashed the door planks with the stumps.

'I was reeking of blood when I regained consciousness. Yes, blood. There was blood on the floor. Blood on the tip of the chisel, blood on the severed fingers, blood on the palms. The blood soaked dress was like red silk. The smell of my own blood, its cold sensation. Whoo! But that was not the end of it. I still wanted to paint her. Where is she? I searched for her. I wrote her name with blood on the walls. I was trying to entice her with a sacrifice. The nude beauty. Do you know, they were all apprehensive that I would complete the picture. The conceited, jealous artists! To prevent that from happening they shut me up within four walls. Forced me to imbibe the medicines and tablets prescribed by the pigs. But I continued to draw her even when I was locked up. Didn't I tell you, in the canvas of my mind. But she is a *yakshi* whom I could not paint successfully despite innumerable attempts. Finally, I lost. I was a moth that got singed in the flame of a lamp.' He was panting.

'I failed. But it does not matter to me. The defeated are by far greater in numbers than the victors. I will manage to live the life of an animal keeping accounts and typing with index fingers. However, there is one sure thing, I will not let anyone becoming great by painting her picture,' He paused menacingly.

'If she is portrayed I will make mincemeat of them. Just as they did of me.'

He banged the wooden panels again with the stump of his left palm.

Someone was stirring in the next room.

I did not stay there any longer. On my way back too, the two dogs on the alley got up and made way for me. When I reached the road I heard the shattering sound of something that was hurled out, from behind.

Next morning Monayi was there waiting for me. He behaved as if nothing of significance had happened the previous night.

'I want some money.' He said, 'I will repay it by working. It is urgent. Medicines to be bought.'

I gave him half of what he asked for.

In the evening he came again, fully drunk. Monayi shouted at me when he was told that I will not give him any more money.

'I know that you have an eye on the girl. Not for painting but for writing about. To portray. Pigs!' some of my acquaintances had come to the office for making deposits and I got wild.

'Don't talk rubbish,' I shouted.

'There is nothing that is rubbish on earth, my friend. Everything has its own use.' He smiled, 'Who has not eyed her?'

'You need not come here anymore, if it is going to be like this,' I said.

He remained indecisive for a while and then left.

Monayi never returned. A small ad appeared in the local rag for Dayal Investments: 'A reputed financial institution requires an experienced typist'.

'The conclusion of a manuscript,' I thought.

In course of time other periodicals too published my stories. But I did not bother to publish a collection as Monayi had wanted. That was a time when there were no publishers for short stories. The short novel which he had brought was written after I left that place; in fact, after many years. He was not there in my mind when I wrote it. As also, my old job and the ambience of that place. The novel was about two old masons.

I had left the job at the end of the contracted three years. I got into another one in this town after being unemployed for a short period. Everything the palmist had predicted about me had come true. Maybe she had mentioned only such things that could be deduced by mere commonsense. And maybe because it was not of any relevance, she had not gone into my literary career.

However, an advertisement that appeared in the newspapers years after leaving that place seemed to round off her predictions.

The Reserve Bank, while bringing in restrictions on non banking financial institutions had also published a table of blacklisted companies. It was in the form of a notification.

It was published with prominence in most of the newspapers and I did not miss the name 'Dayal Investments', though it was in extremely small print.

I did not try to read that letter sitting in the cabin. Excusing myself I went to my seat and as I opened the letter I remembered Monayi saying that he was good material for a novel.

I tried to read it as the epilogue of a big story. It was not long. Just a few lines, in beautiful handwriting.

Dear friend,

I write this with the hope that you remember me. I had come to meet you and to renew our friendship. And also to express my happiness in knowing that you have written a novel. I made a search for it and read it. I had expected that this old artist would appear at least in a minor role in your novel. But it was not there. You must include me in the next—at least in a small role. I'm on leave for a few days. 'Parole' is the word here.

Don't you remember? There was the stench of blood on my hands. It was blood again that lead me here.

Yes, that old woman had smelled blood on my hands—the blood of another.

Who can condone that? That was why she had driven me away.

There was a strange serenity on her face when she lay there with blood draining from her. She had certainly surpassed many great nude portraits. Like in the portrait of Venus, an unearthly beauty was glowing from her. Something melancholic. She was like a sleeping beauty.

There is no sight more heartbreaking than of those sleeping in the nude.

Then, then, for the first time I had empathy for her.

Truthfully, she was an innocent being…

Yours,
Joseph Monayi

When I reached his name, three severed fingers were thrashing about like fish inside me.

And that small piece of paper began to tremble as if it was caught in a wild wind.

~

Another Summer

Everyone was ready with bag and baggage even before the bus had arrived at the last stop. A queue had already formed to the exit door. Raghu joined them.

Sunanda had also got up from the seat along with him. But she had lingered there for some more time. The bus had reached the station by then. While on the last step, he turned around and looked for her. Sunanda was not there behind him. He retraced his steps. She was leaning on the seat.

'Why, did you forget anything?' he asked loudly.

'Oh, nothing,' She shrugged. She was the last to get out of the bus.

While waiting for an autorickshaw, she whispered for his ears only, 'Blood'.

~

They had been travelling through the night. Raghu looked around with tired eyes as they got out of the bus station. It was already bright. The day was warm.

It was an overnight journey from their place to town B. The bus left in the evening to reach B in the morning.

They had booked early and so had got adjacent seats. Raghu recalled their first journey to town B, 20 years ago. They were in the back row of seats in the bus and it was so cramped. They had just got married. A hurriedly arranged honeymoon trip at the insistence of their friends. They stayed in the town for the first two days, frequented the park and ice cream parlour, had noodles and mushroom curry in a dimly lit Chinese restaurant, saw a movie in an alien language and went to a hill station three hours from B and returned on the same day. They had the feeling that they had not seen enough of the town and so wandered about on the streets and the vast grounds. It was the first time for them on an escalator. They visited the huge malls dotting the town, just for the heck of riding the escalator and stared at the glass windows of the shops crammed with all the magical things of the world. They had returned by train. In those days they could overcome the stress and strains of the journey by endlessly talking about a myriad of subjects. He had vague memories of all of it even now. Distant memories, as if all that had happened in another birth. Sunanda however, did not seem to have any inkling of any of it.

Now, despite sitting next to each other on the same seat, they hardly talk to each other and travel almost like strangers. Raghu was worn out, maybe because he had not slept well the previous night. But slumber kept away because the patterns of his day were disturbed. He sat back on his seat with his eyes closed. He was aware that Sunanda too was sitting just like him, with sleep keeping away. A Hindi movie was being shown on the video screen and it went on till late at night. Lights from outside peeped into the bus occasionally, as if emphasising that it was indeed dark.

Two different types of towns at the two proximities of a night. Raghu tried to imagine that they were traversing through a long tunnel of darkness.

Later on, at some point of time, he fell asleep. It was almost six when he woke up.

The outside world was not yet lucid through the dusty windows. Raghu saw that darkness was still hovering around on the roads, as if a great shadow had fallen. He could read the distance to town B on some of the illuminated boards. Darkness returned. The bus was now running through deserted fallow lands. And a little later he could see the boards with the names of the streets in town B. The bus was then slowly passing by the rain trees which were stooping and looking into themselves in the scanty light of the early morning. Endless rows of rain trees was the feature of town B.

Maybe they are the same trees of their first visit, only older. Beyond that everything else was strange. Huge new bridges that had come about across the roads on tall pillars, a new clock tower, multi-storey buildings, broad roads not crowded as yet because it was still early morning, vehicles gliding away like boats on water; the town grew up in his vision maintaining a distance of 20 years. This cannot be the old town, Raghu felt. The feeling that they had been here earlier, maybe it was merely a feeling.

~

'Blood,' she repeated. 'It is all over the seat. Oh, what will they think…'

'What will they think?' Raghu said. 'Where are we going to meet them again? And such things happen. They will wash and clean it.'

They did not talk for a while. Autorickshaw drivers were reluctant when they heard the destination. It is far away. Little chances of getting a return trip.

'I feel terribly wet and blotted,' Sunanda said, 'Let's rent a room somewhere nearby.'

'But the doctor's clinic is quite far from here,' Raghu said. 'We have already booked a room in a hotel near the clinic, isn't it? Going to the clinic will be easier.'

'I can't wait till then. My back is all wet.'

'You did not use pads?'

'You don't understand,' Sunanda looked at him, agitatedly. 'Is it because I do not use pads? It is just not enough. It is like a rain. I am all soaked. I have to get rid of these pads before people start noticing.'

He was sweating profusely, however. 'The climate of this place has changed,' Raghu commented, settling down in the auto. 'In the olden days fans were not required here even in summer. Big buildings, big roads, vehicles have taken over; rain and mist have vanished.'

Sunanda did not respond. She was trying to keep her body elevated from the seat by a posture between sitting and standing.

Raghu noticed a new world blooming on the billboards in the city. Jewellery, smart phones, branded clothes for men and women, villas and flats, soda water with the same names as liquor, mineral water, movies. Dazzling models with desirable figures representing undergarments and condoms. He stole a glance at them. Usually when they come across such ads, Sunanda would keenly observe him. She would notice his eyes quickly sweeping across the billboard.

'Chhee … these men are shameless,' she would say in an accusing tone. 'Why do you stare at them?'

'I was only reading the phone number alongside,' Raghu would blurt out, averting his gaze.

'Ayyo … why do you lie like this! Phone number … You watch and enjoy. I don't bother! But don't come out with such fabrications. These pictures and ads are for shameless fellows like you!'

'You are right', Raghu would laugh. 'These ad men will be reduced to begging if at least a few like me do not glance at them.' But today she did not notice anything.

He cancelled the hotel booking made earlier and was now looking for a room close by, as suggested by Sunanda. The auto driver stopped in front of a small hotel.

'Not this,' Raghu said. 'This looks like a matchbox.'

'This will do.' Sunanda was already getting out with the suitcase. 'We need only minimum facilities. Maximum one week. And it will be over in a jiffy.' Raghu stopped protesting.

'In a small room during these warm days! There is not even sufficient light,' Raghu said, trying to open the window, pushing aside the soiled curtain. 'Why not take an A/C room? I cannot put up with heat and dust any more. You know I'm allergic. Once I start sneezing, there is no end to it. And at present we can afford it too. When we could not, we adjusted to that kind of living.'

'I don't want anything more than this. Not in the sight of anyone and not seeing anyone; a place where I can be alone. I need only that much for now.' Sunanda placed the suitcase on the bed and hurried to the bathroom.

'Where are the switches? Raghu peered at the walls. He feared that darkness was slouching in the room like an invisible animal. When he attempted to open the window, its hinges creaked into a moan. Must be ages since it was opened last. When he managed to open one shutter, it became obvious why it was never opened. A large building stood very close by, preventing light or air from coming in.

When he finally located the switch and put the light on, it was quite insufficient. The animal that was darkness merely shifted to a more discreet corner—that was all.

~

Raghu had arranged an appointment two weeks ago with the famed doctor in city B. He remitted the consultation fee through the Internet.

Sunanda had insisted that they come to this city for a consultation. If not here, then at a similar place. As far away from their home town as possible. A city where no one would recognise them, or bother about them. He could not understand that. The hospitals in their town had all the facilities for any kind of investigations. The journey, accommodation and all related hardships were being taken on for nothing. But Sunanda insisted.

'Are you afraid that others would come to know?' Raghu asked.

'It is not really fear. It's something else. Sort of a complex. I'm afraid of not just others, I fear my body too,' Sunanda said. They were returning after meeting the gynaecologist for the first time. 'I don't understand it, my body. Till now I could feel its warmth or coldness just by touch. Now it is behaving like a stranger's body,' she had said regretfully.

'I've become used to people. They are all known to us since long. I also know what kind of questions they ask,' Sunanda said. And that was the fact. She was quite familiar with the questions regarding the treatment and the medicines, the normal queries faced by couples without children. Advice and recommendations about various treatment methods, sympathy, and rarely ridiculing too. That had all become sort of routine. But that was not the issue now. 'I fail when I encounter this body of mine,' she continued. 'I feel it is not under my control. I get confused not knowing how it is going to behave.'

'What's it with your body?' Raghu asked. He was getting irritated. 'There is slight bleeding these days, isn't it? Doctor said it is quite natural at this age. Maybe a sort of rush before it ceases altogether…'

'Let it cease. That is what I too would like now. But that is not my problem. You know how regular it was. I was a clock that ticked for 28 days. That accurate. And then the certainty of four days' absolute chaos.'

Sunanda would get ready by circling those four days in red in advance. That is a reminder for him. Red alert. Here, these four red days. Don't even think of talking to me on those days.

Raghu smiled, thinking of those days.

Sunananda said, 'I know why you are smiling. See, those days were indeed disastrous for me. I was furious against everyone. It was a sort of vengeance. My body boiled like a metal solution. Then it would cool and freeze like a snowbound lake. During all that time I did not want to see anyone and wanted to be alone, withdrawing into myself.'

Raghu visualised a rain tree with its leaves folded up.

Gradually he became familiar with all this. Tablets, tonics, ayurvedic medicines and the strict diets. But yet those days recurred. Barren seasons. Same days, same routine. Sunanda remained aloof like a pilgrim travelling into oneself.

All that changed suddenly three months ago. The red circles on the calendar became meaningless. One day, two, three days. 'Nothing happening. Is it that the treatment of yesteryears is finally bearing fruit at this late age?' Raghu exclaimed half-jokingly, but half seriously. Sunanda did not laugh. She understood that for the first time her body was speaking a language she did not understand. On the third evening Raghu fixed up an appointment with the doctor for the next morning. But her body responded that night as if in remorse. The flow was not stopping. He remembers that night when frustration, fear and insult overpowered her. Both of them remained awake through the night. In the morning she stopped him as he was getting the car keys to take her to the doctor. No need to go. Everything seems to be alright now.

'Still let's go. What if something like yesterday happens again?'

'We'll see to it then.'

'Or we will go at the appointed time.'

'No. Bleeding is over anyway. I'm exhausted. I'd like to sleep.'

Raghu stopped for a second on his way to the office, looking at Sunanada curled up in a corner of the bed. Her pale eyelids were throbbing as if she was having a nightmare.

~

Sleeping is no solution for anything. It merely keeps the outside world concealed from us for some time. When she woke up the same springs became active in Sunanda.

In the evening Raghu took Sunanda to the doctor's house, ignoring her objections. The doctor was an elderly lady. She allowed consultation only for those whom she knew from the early days or only unavoidable cases. She mentioned that she was planning to stop that too. If she continues to live there, patients will keep on coming and it will be difficult to say no. She might go abroad to her daughter who has been asking her for long. 'One could rest there, unlike here,' she said. She patiently heard Sunanda, asked her a few questions, checked her BP and temperature. 'Start these medicines for the time being. We have to go for some tests.'

'Sometimes the uterus may have to be removed, isn't it doctor?' Raghu raised the question, based on what little he knew.

'Yes, but that is just a minor thing. But I suspect … the side effects of medicines taken or sometimes … she stopped midway. Don't worry, we will do some tests.' Then she mentioned the name of another doctor. 'You see him also. I'll call and tell him.'

'Who is he?' Raghu asked, thinking about Sunanda's hesitation in consulting a male gynaecologist.

Don't worry.' The doctor smiled. 'He is a young man. Brilliant. Classmate of my son. He is like my son.' She looked at him and added, 'He is aware of all the latest developments. I don't keep myself that up-to-date.'

'Why doctor, anything…'

'No, no, nothing like that. Just to check for any growth or so … Just to rule out the possibility. That's all. Meet him.'

The medicines she prescribed were effective in the beginning. But gradually Sunanda's body managed to overcome them. Clocks wavered as if mad. She became familiar with bleeding that could happen on any day, at any time. It also stopped as suddenly as it started. Her calendar became a garden of red flowers.

They went to the young doctor recommended by the lady gynaecologist. Certain medicines, a scan and consult him again after a week.

'We will test, yes that is what I'm trying to do.' On the second visit, the doctor tried to console him. Raghu had not taken Sunanda with him. The doctor continued, 'I was checking the medicines taken by your wife in the past. She was taking a large dose. Just google and see. Many of them are banned abroad. Europe had stopped the production of most of them almost 30 years ago. I am wondering whether this is the effect of all those medicines.'

'But Doctor, you have not told me what exactly happened,' Raghu reminded him.

'For that a thorough check up will have to be done. The scan report is here,' he said taking out a file. 'There's a growth. It is very clear. Moreover, it has spread beyond the uterus. But to what extent it is serious and other details will not be available in this report. A biopsy will have to be done.'

'Biopsy? Then…' Raghu hesitated. 'When is it to be done?'

'It can be done anytime,' the doctor said. 'But the bleeding has to be under control. Otherwise the result will not be clear. I'll make the prescription then. It will take one week for the result.'

When he got up to leave, the doctor said, 'No need to mention any of this to your wife right now. It is quite possible that there will not be anything to bother after this test. We can remove this growth through a minor surgery.'

Raghu accepted that advice. 'Maybe there is nothing serious. Perhaps there may be some kind of swelling. That will subside,' he told Sunanda, as if nothing of consequence has happened.

'It cannot be that way,' Sunanda disagreed. 'That young doctor might not have diagnosed properly.'

'What is there to be diagnosed with great accuracy?' Raghu was irritated. Then he paused and said, 'Let's have another test done.'

'I can't. I can't go to the same place again. People will notice.'

'Let them notice. It was you who said that you are now used to the questions people ask?'

'It's not that. I don't want to face anyone now. They will all think that we are still on the course for a child.'

'What people think is nothing to us. This is a matter affecting only you and me.'

Still Sunanda did not yield. 'We'll go to another place, a place no one knows, no one notices. I'll be more up to it, in such a place. There is no better shield than the crowd of strangers.

At last, after long deliberations and enquiries they had settled down on city B.

To the city of rain trees, standing lonely in the crowd, withdrawn into themselves.

~

On their first day in city B Sunanda just lay on the bed the whole day. She felt much better by evening. She slept well in the night.

Next morning, they went to the doctor at the appointed time. The tests were done and samples taken. On the way back, Sunanda asked, 'Are you are getting bored?'

He did not reply. He was sitting on the bed trying to read a book. But he was not able to concentrate.

'Why are you sitting here guarding me like a genie?' she asked, a smile flashing on her lips. 'Go out. There will be many things to see here now. We noticed on the way, no, what a lot of changes. You can even spend time walking around.'

'Won't you feel lonely?' Raghu asked.

'That does not matter. I don't like to go out. But you carry on. How long will you sit here? And now there are all kinds of facilities. If there is anything, I'll call on the mobile.'

'That's true. It is not like the former times. One can return at any time because of the cell phone.'

Before leaving the room he asked, 'Shall we make a trip to Puttaparthi or Tirupati?

Sunanda laughed. 'When did you become a devotee?'

'Not because of that. Didn't we leave our home town citing these places as our destination? It will take four or five days for the results. We can go if we want, that's all.'

'No,' Sunanda was firm. 'Devotion has not come to our aid when we needed it. I just cannot go to any ashram and sing bhajans.'

He did not respond.

'But you can go if you feel like, ok?' Sunanda said after a pause. 'I'm not afraid to be alone.'

'No, I did not mean to go on my own.'

'Then why not make a tour of this city? Everything has changed. You will not feel that you have been here before.'

As Raghu was leaving, she looked at him keenly and asked, 'You must hate me now, eh?'

He looked at her. Her eyes were sorrowful. He did not answer.

'I'm all in pieces. My body is gone. Of what use is it, anymore?'

He too was aware of it. It had been weeks since he had even touched her. Many nights he was haunted by the helpless lament of his body. He used to feel the inception of unwarranted hatred between them at such moments.

'If I die,' she asked him without any change in her expressions, 'If I die, will you marry again?'

'You will not die,' he declared with conviction. 'At least not before I die.'

'You did not answer my question,' she laughed.

'What is it that you want?' he became restless.

'You should get married. That is my wish. You should have children in that marriage,' Sunanda said in measured tones. 'And not like in old movies, the tragic hero with long hair and unkempt beard … No.'

'Do you want anything when I come back?' he tried to change the subject.

'No. I don't need anything. Go for a movie.' And then she continued with a mysterious smile. 'Gaze at young men and young women. Stare at those ads in peace.'

~

In the bus to the city centre Raghu was thinking about what Sunanda had said. Perhaps her anxiety might not be about his boredom. Privacy is her first priority these days. Her preference is to be alone, dwelling deep into herself. Anything else and everyone else breaches her aloneness. Her misgivings, even if he was only a little late coming home in the evening, have faded away. Everyone else became alien to her in her attempts to nurse her body, which was like a disobedient grown-up child. An enormous hell consisting of aliens surrounded her little universe.

Raghu loitered through city B, scanning the skyscrapers that dotted the streets. Then he saw metro trains in the distance. He turned in that direction. Going down the staircase to the underground metro station he purchased a ticket to the third station. It was not the peak hour and most of the seats were vacant. Getting down at the third station he reached the ground level, going up the stairs. That seemed to be the centre of city B. The streets seemed to be bursting at the seams because of the burgeoning crowds. Vehicles sped past in all directions without any break, coming to a halt for a little while at the traffic signals. There was a cloudless dreary sky and it was a hot day.

He saw a group of girls crossing the road. All of them were in clinging jeans and T-shirts. The T-shirts sported slogans. They were not legible from a distance. Books in their hands, bags on shoulders, they could be college students. Or they may be attending coaching classes or may even be working in call centres. He stood there on the footpath watching them. The red digits on the traffic signal decreased.

The girls crossed to his side of the road and walked past him along the footpath. He turned like a mechanical doll. Their pace had slowed down due to the swelling crowd. His eyes sharpened on their dance-like steps. Raghu stood there watching them till they were lost in the distance. Slightly higher, the dazzling beauty of the billboard displaying winked at him.

The traffic lights had turned green. The unusual boom of the horns woke him up to the immediate present. He was in a dilemma, which direction should he take…

~

'Hello, why are you standing here like this?' a young woman asked Raghu, touching his shoulder. He turned around. 'Who is this talking to me in such a familiar tone in this city?'

She did not seem to be an acquaintance. 'Or is it that I have seen her somewhere, but cannot recollect. Or is she someone I had wished to see?'

'Don't suck the blood of those girls with your gaze. Poor girls, let them live for some more years,' she said with a smile.

'She must have noticed that I was standing there all this while staring at those girls,' he thought to himself. He was embarrassed. He looked at her like an idiot.

'Doesn't matter.' She winked at him. 'I was just joking. And this is just fun after all, no?'

'Have we met?' Raghu asked.

'Have we?' she looked at him roguishly. 'Perhaps … No, I don't think so. But it doesn't matter even if we have not met. We can get acquainted no? When I saw one of our own folk standing in the street and counting the girls, I thought, why not just head in. Is there anything wrong in it?'

She must be around 25, he made a guess. Goggles with big black glasses. Lips shining with lipstick. Henna-coloured hair cropped at shoulder level. She too was wearing a T-shirt, its neckline going deep into her cleavage. The slogan on the T-shirt says 'I'm Dirty, My Dear'. Faded blue jeans, cut at the right knee. 'Who is she?' Raghu had absolutely no idea.

'Let's take a walk if you have time,' she said. She looked at him, removing her glasses and wiping it with her handkerchief. She has a strange kind of beauty, he felt. Flaming beauty. Those sparkling laughing eyes sent a silent invitation.

He did not answer, but started walking by her side.

~

'Your first time here?' she asked.

'No.'

Raghu did not elaborate. This was not the city he had seen on the first visit, he felt. Buildings, roads, vehicles and bill boards … all have changed. Even people have changed.

'Stand like this with your mouth agape on the street and someone will flick you away, she laughed. 'Or at least pick your pocket.'

'I was waiting for the traffic signal to…' Raghu tried to explain. Then he gave up. Another row of girls passed them by.

'Where are you from, in Kerala?' she enquired. He mentioned his native place.

'Shall we go somewhere and sit down for some time?' she suggested. 'Let's not wander about on this hot day. I'm free till the evening. If you have time to spare…'

He looked at her. He felt he could see a sliver of naughtiness flashing on her face. She was wearing a small steel chain with a blue locket. The image on the locket was not clearly visible. She was behaving like an old friend, Raghu thought. But he still had his doubts.

'Where to sit?' he thought. 'We can go to a park,' he suggested.

'But there is no such park nearby. Moreover who will go to a park at this noon hour?' She paused looking straight at him, 'Why not go to a pub?'

'Pub…'

'Why master, scared? A beer will cool you down. Why, you don't drink beer?'

'Once in a while. But…'

'No buts! Go straight. Only few steps and there is a pub at the turning. There will not be any rush.'

~

The pub's interior was segmented into cabins. An old but neat place. The dragon on the wall reminded Raghu of the Chinese restaurant where Sunanda and he had dinner, the first time they had come to city B. Dim light and western music at a fast tempo. It was disturbingly loud. They went into a vacant cabin and sat side by side. He had first sat on a chair opposite to her. But she pointed to the seat next to her and asked him to sit there saying, 'We can hear each other only if we sit close by. Listen, it is acid rock. And my head numbs from this kind of stereo sound.'

'Two cans of beer,' she ordered without asking him. When the bearer left, she took his hand in hers and gently patted it. Raghu looked straight into her eyes. He felt the levels of music rising yet again. She looked at him and laughed loudly and pressed his palm.

'Why are you sitting still? What happened to the gusto you showed on the road?' She asked, tilting the beer can into her mouth.

Raghu merely looked at her with an awkward grin. He tasted the beer and kept the can on the table.

'I can easily recognise the people I come across,' she said. Raghu remained silent.

She blew into her T shirt and continued, 'How hot it is even in this A/C room!' He peeped through the cleavage of the T-shirt to have a glance of her breasts.

'Oh, what are you looking at?' she asked mischievously. Raghu didn't know what to reply.

'These words,' gathering courage he asked her, looking at her breasts, 'Why these words like this?'

'What about it?'

This 'I'm Dirty, My Dear…'

'Because I'm dirty!' she said, very casually.

'Is it so?' He became helpless, not getting the apt words.

'My silly guy, this T-shirt is supplied by traders. Is it I who has written these words? Drink that beer. You are showing all symptoms of not having it.'

He gulped the full can in one swig. She ordered one more each for both of them. And then softly took his hands.

~

Two cans of beer later Raghu became bolder. He ran his fingers over her jeans and pressed her thighs. She was going through the menu card. She pretended to be unaware of his doings. Her smooth body enhanced his intoxication. He clutched her thighs vigorously.

'Hey what is this!' She released his grip and said as if scolding him. 'Skin will come off master!'

Taking away his hand from her thigh, he touched her shoulders and neck, softly.

'Yes, behave like a good boy,' she said. 'What are we going to order for food?'

'You order whatever you fancy.'

'Why, don't you have any preferences?'

'It is you I prefer.' There was a bit of coyness in his voice. 'I want to savour a dirty girl along with my beer.'

'Smart! getting into top gear!' … Suddenly she kissed him on his cheek.

'Whenever I come here, I go for a special dish,' she said.

'What is it?'

'Dragon chicken.' She pointed to the drawing of dragon on the wall. 'Look, the dragon is a smart guy. It will be hot. But a beer will take care of it.'

'Let it be dragon, if your choice is dragon.' Raghu continued perching on the steps of intoxication. 'I too like it hot.' He brought his palm to the top of her T-shirt.

'Sho! My dear master, let me tell you a truth, you do not know how to deal with women. This is like a JCB closing in for excavation. How lecherous you are!'

'Ok. Then tell me how to behave with women.' Raghu did not withdraw his hand from her breast.

'That,' she said folding the menu. 'Woman is like a glass vessel. You cannot jump on it. It will break. See, very, very soft dealings only.' As if to demonstrate, she inserted her hand inside his shirt and moved her long fingers on his chest slowly. He trembled in excitement.

'Ayyo, I forgot to ask, you have money with you, no?' she withdrew her hand and looked at him.

'Why do you ask me such a question?'

'Please do not take it wrong. I had thought of drawing from the ATM on my way. But then we got in here. This pub is quite expensive. We'll get a fat bill.'

'Oh, bill … so that's your worry! Is 2,000 on the higher side?' He took out his purse from his pocket. 'See, about 3,000 in cash! And an ATM card. If necessary that can be used. Enough?'

'Oh master mine! You are…' she took the purse, opened it casually and continued. 'Tut … tut. Did I ask you to show your purse and convince me? It is just like our people from back home. It is all exhibition once they go out.'

'I speak only the truth,' Raghu said.

'Here, keep it back.' She stared at him playfully returning the purse. 'These days no one carries cash, isn't it? All card and net now. Hey master, this card here, is there something in it? Or just one for namesake?'

'Come on now. Always joking eh? This is a card with cash. Don't worry. You place the order for dragon chicken.'

'Why place an order?' She laughed with delight. 'A real dragon is sitting by my side, no!'

Raghu laughed as if he had heard a delightful joke.

~

They remained in the pub for some more time after settling the bill.

'Tell me, just whiling away our time eating dragon, will it do for the day?'

'Shouldn't we really celebrate?' she asked.

'Yes, indeed. I was about to suggest that.'

'So what's the programme? Are you familiar with this place?'

'No,' Raghu said.

'Where do you stay? Any hotel?'

'No.' Raghu came out with a lie. 'With a friend…'

'Then let's take a room,' she suggested.

'In a hotel? Yes.'

'No, let's not do that.' She seemed to deliberate. 'That might turn out to be a problem later on. I'm known to many here. I work here, no?'

'You work?'

'Then what? Did you think I enjoy a carefree life eating dragon and drinking beer? That's indeed fine. Now look, I work in a call centre. Eight years.'

'Okay, so no hotel then.' There was a tiny note of disappointment in Raghu's tone.

'Oh, won't it be awful if someone sees me?'

'But what do we do then?' Raghu looked at her. 'Forgot to ask you, what's your name?'

'My name?' That can wait. What's your name?'

Raghu thought for a while. There is no need to tell his name. Not the real name anyway. Why not Raghu Raman instead of Raghu Nandanan? But then as if prompted by something else, he said, 'It is Raman, Ramachandran.'

She burst out laughing. 'When they reach this stage, everyone has only this name: Raman. All Indians are Raman.' She seemed to be tickled.

'What is your name?'

'Sita,' She said in a serious tone. He too laughed now.

~

The sun seemed to be too hot as they came out of the pub. His eyes folded up on entering light from darkness. The rush on the roads had increased. They walked slowly along the footpath.

'If so Rametta, chhe, that is not it: Raman, yes, Raman, let's do it differently. We need not go to any hotel or resort. They will milk you quoting exotic rent. No need for any of that! Here, there's a building that I know within walking distance. A friend of mine has a room there. She comes there only once in a while. I have one key with me. Why not go and rest there?'

He nodded.

'Then follow me. Someone could be hanging around there. Just ignore them. You walk behind me. We are not acquainted any more, ok? Two persons who do not know each other walking into that building separately. Will it not work out?'

He nodded again.

'It has to. If not you can straight away go back. Thank you for your beer and dragon chicken. And for your friendship.'

'I will come,' Raghu said.

'If so, give me a 500 rupee note.'

He looked at her with uncertainty.

'That is my fees,' she said.

'Fees!' Raghu hesitated for a moment.

'Then what did you think? Five hundred rupees. I'll not take more from you. But you have to pay in advance. Men just duck away once what they want is attained! Not trustworthy.' She continued while laughing, 'And no need to take out all the contents of that purse for a 500 rupee note. All are not like me. Some one will snatch it if they see.'

Obediently, he put his hand in his trouser pocket and gave her a note.

'Good boy,' she said poking his cheek. 'No, good Raman!'

~

She stepped down to the left just before the deviation to the metro station. It was a small path. Shops reaching out on to the road, pavement hawkers, flock of goats and cows listlessly looking into the distance: he could see how the city's character changes by stepping down a mere foot. People huddled at various points: in front of the cobbler, in front of the tinker, the indigenous medicine man, the old book seller ... She walked past them without even a side glance. She seemed to know the way like the lines on her palm, Raghu thought.

He walked behind her. But at some point he lost her. He scanned for her on either side of the road. Turned around and looked behind. Finally he resumed walking forward, thinking, 'Come what may'.

But she was not to be seen even after quite some distance. Doubts crept in. He had heard many stories about girls in this city befriending men, having food and drinks, swindling some money and vanishing. They would be having jobs alright, but employ such tricks to live lavishly. Doesn't matter. At least there is the consolation that no one is aware of this folly. He decided to go back in the direction he had come from.

'Hey master … here!' She was hailing him from some distance ahead. Yes, it was her alright. Waving at him, standing near the entrance of a big building.

~

It was a very old building. Greenish tan of weeds on the cracked walls. Windows of the rooms in the three floors opening out like stretched hands. Some of them hanging on to the hinges. Few old vehicles parked on the small courtyard in front of the building. Most of them appeared to be dilapidated. Many of them did not have tyres. Seemed to be a place for abandoned vehicles.

As he reached the entrance she said slowly, 'Here, our way is from behind this building. You come after I'm gone for sometime. You should not hesitate. There may be some people loitering around. Don't mind them.'

He grunted. His beer induced high was gradually coming down. A notion that the whole thing was avoidable seemed to be creeping in.

How about asking her to leave? Let her take that 500. That does not matter. Can't follow her like a thief any more. He blamed himself for entering into such a venture.

But then the sensation of her touch came back to him. Her aroma, her soft body, the slender fingers caressing his chest. Her shapely breasts he saw through the V of her T-shirt … He followed her slowly and softly, like a cat.

~

Bottles, old and rusted metallic parts and broken vessels were heaped behind the building. He was enveloped by the overpowering stench of urine. The whole place seemed to be deserted.

There was a spiralling iron staircase to the left. She reached the bottom of the stairs and then there was the sound of someone else talking. He saw her going up the stairs. Raghu reached the staircase.

Three youths—or perhaps middle aged—were smoking sitting on the lowest steps of the staircase. They were talking and laughing intermittently. Their language was different, Raghu noticed. They were clean shaven short guys. All three of them had the look of youths from the north-east working as waiters in Chinese restaurants.

One of them shifted a bit, making way for him to go up. Otherwise all of them ignored him totally. They seemed to be immersed in their smoking and jokes. She was opening the shutter of a small room to the left of the staircase. She then raised the shutter and got in, bending her body.

'Come, get in,' she said. He bent low and followed her. The sounds the young men were making down below still reached him.

As soon as he was fully inside, she lowered the shutter. Suddenly the room was stuffed with darkness. Nothing was visible. He remained there for sometime like a blind man unable to see even the immediate surroundings.

Then he heard the sound of a key turning at the bottom end of the shutter.

'What is it?' he asked.

'I just locked it. Don't worry. It is to prevent anyone else from sneaking in.'

'No light?' he floundered.

'Light for what?' she laughed again. There is no power supply in this room.

He panicked.

'Don't worry. I'll find a way out.' She opened a window. A slice of light entered the room bisecting the darkness. He had a look around in the dim light. It was a tiny room. There was an old cot in one corner with a mat, a pillow and a crumpled bed sheet. A packet of candles on the small table. A couple of folded dresses. The room itself was divided by a half wall. The other side was another room. It could have been a bathroom. That too was unlit. The stench of urine seemed to be omnipresent.

'Tired walking?' she asked with obvious naughtiness. 'Oh, for this specific purpose men are ready to go to any black hole, no?'

He just stared at her with a stupid smile.

'See, there's no time to stand and stare. What happened to the excitement you had when you were gaping at those girls! Be a good boy and remove your clothes.'

He hesitated.

She closed in on him and languidly undid the buttons of his shirt. Undoing the zip, she pulled down his trousers. Standing there in his undergarments, he crossed his arms across his chest like children do.

She fished out his cell phone from his shirt pocket and examined it. 'Oh, this is a new cell, master? It's smart, eh?' She placed it in her palm and looked at it as if weighing it. Then placed it carefully on the table. His trousers were the next. She searched both the pockets. Examined the purse and placed that too on the table.

Then she slowly rolled the trousers and the shirt together and made a ball of it. Then she threw it beyond the half wall in the room.

Only then did it dawn upon Raghu that he had been done in well and truly. The last drop of intoxication oozed out of him.

~

'You are not Raman, you are only a "day Raman". But my dear day Raman-master, you are an awful miser. I've got to say that. Coming to such a big city and yet walking about with a measly 3,000 in your purse … Chee … even I am ashamed. But then I had a gut feeling that you are not a trouble maker. That was why I invited you here. Still you lied to me. Doesn't matter.'

'I told you nothing but the truth,' his voice quivered.

'Cool, cool, my dear. That is no big issue. Anyone would lie. A lie is also truth. Lying is another method of telling the truth, isn't it? And this was only a small lie.'

'What was it?'

'That is … your name is Raghunandan, right?'

'How … how…' he stammered. 'Do you really know me?'

'Hey, never. Then the question is: How did I come to know? Very simple. Whose name will be printed on the ATM card, if not yours? I just saw it.'

'See, please don't harm me. You can take whatever is left in the purse. But my clothes … please give them back. I will go away. Please…'

'No, no, eh … I never harm anyone. Why did we take all this trouble to get here? Buck up man! We'll go only after celebrating.'

He stood there staring at her, words eluding him.

She opened his purse and showed him its contents. Maybe there is about 400 left. That's all. That is simply not sufficient for me. It is pretty tough to live in this city. People are throwing money around. Small cash won't do for even ordinary living. Who wants to listen to explanations?'

She pulled out his ATM card from the purse. 'Will there be some amount in this card of Raghunandanan? What is the PIN?'

He thought of Sunanda. A lumpsum meant for her treatment had been deposited in the bank. If she has her way, the entire money will be swiped out. Raghu just looked at her and remained standing.

'Now, open out. As of now it is a matter between just the two of us. It will be over this moment. But if you don't give the PIN, others will truck in. Do you see three vagabonds sitting at the bottom of the staircase. Only good for eating. And so quite healthy. Actually I don't like them. But if you want to survive in a place like this, one has to bear with such rascals. No other way. Tell me the PIN of this card…'

He mumbled a four-digit number.

'Ok,' she said after repeating the number once. 'Listen master, sure you have not gone wrong? Suppose this number is not correct, the card will get locked after three tries. Then you have to wait for 24 hours before it is set right. You will have to be here till then. I warned you no, you can't go from here till we get the money. I badly require money. And even if I relent, those dwarfs sitting outside will not let you go.'

He said hesitantly, 'That number is wrong.'

'I thought so,' she smiled. 'Doesn't matter. I explained to you what would happen otherwise. Now come out with it.'

Raghu mentioned the correct number and stared at her with hatred.

She took the card, walked up to the open window and called out loudly, '*Are* Kishore, *zara idhar aa. Ye card lo, aur paisa nikaalkar fatafat aa jaana* (Kishore, come here. Take this card, withdraw money and come back quickly).

She waited for the person and then, handing over the card, said, '*Der math kar,* Kishore. *Idhar udhar dekhkar ganja peekar time barbad math karna. Saab ko jaldi jaana hai nad'* (Don't waste time, Kishore. Don't hang about gaping at shop windows or smoking ganja. The saheb here, wants to leave early).

He may have gone down just two steps when she called again. 'Kishore, *poore ka poore balans nikaalna math. Kuch to baaki rakhna. Minimam balans. Han, our ek bat. Rasiid mujhe dikhaana. Kuch gadbad huyi tho choduungii nahi, samjhaa?'* (Kishore, don't withdraw the entire balance. Keep something there. Minimum balance. And then show me the receipt. I won't spare anyone if anything goes wrong. Understood?).

She came back to him and said, 'They are good for nothing. They sit there the whole day getting high on ganja. They just don't do any work. After all they are mere pimps! You know the standards of the pimps.'

She moved closer to him and continued. 'Really speaking, this bunch here are not even pimps. That's the fun of it. I have to seek out my prey on my own. These fellows are merely lip-licking dogs. I let them be, thinking of them as someone to lean on. Not that I like them a bit.'

She planted a kiss on his cheek and said, 'Ayyo, you are so chilled! Terrified? Wait, no hurry. We will have a merry time once he is back here with money.'

She freed her hands from his body and let her fingers run across his chest. Raghu recalled that she had done so, while they were in the pub. Her long fingers had kindled a fire in him then.

'I'll take this too, ok. Please don't have any grudge towards me.' She pulled off the chain from his neck with a forceful action. Raghu tried to block her.

Ey master! Go slow … don't try to use force. Ok, I got it,' she smiled. 'I had anticipated this at first sight. I confirmed it while sitting in the pub by searching you. Just take a look at the Malayali male of these days! Everyone struts around with chains and bangles and bracelets. Only earrings are missing!' Her laughter boomed.

She examined the gold chain, placing it on her palm. She extended her arm towards the open window, maybe because the light was insufficient. Keeping the chain on the table she embraced him with her arms circling him and whispered into his ears, 'Fantastic! Must be two, two-and-a-half sovereigns?'

He stood as if all senses had deserted him. Her fingers crawled over his body. She seemed to be measuring his face with her lips. But the sensation Raghu had was that of a slimy creature, like a snail, touching him. He was disgusted with his own body.

This is now like embracing an iceberg; she complained moving away from him. Raghu maintained his silence. He felt that time was creeping very slowly, almost like a man handicapped with a heavy weight tied to his leg.

~

The one who had gone to get the money returned after some time. He handed over the cash and the ATM receipt through the window. She counted the notes very carefully and then approached him again.

'Here master, your card. I've kept it safe in the purse. Good going. You are a gentleman. The PIN was correct. Now there's no reason to be afraid. You can go back early, completing your mission. No one would know. I told you no, this is a deal between you and me alone.'

He was standing with bowed head as she got to him. She softly touched his body. Then she extended her hand to his undergarment with a grin. She laughed. He thought she was celebrating his manhood going limp. Was that laughter never going to cease?

'Now now … what happened here for this gloom? All energy oozed out as if struck by arthritis? Is it money matters, eh! A serious ailment or say an accident—all these would drain out your money, isn't it? Why bother so much about it? You can always make money; but will we meet ever again? I like you immensely. And anyway you are knee-deep in water; is it not better to round it off with a bathe? Come, be a good boy and sit on this bed. Ok, I shall close the window if you are feeling shy.'

'Sita,' he called her as she was moving towards the window.

She stopped. 'Sita? That is not my name, you know. But it is alright. What's there in a name, after all!'

'I want to go,' he whispered. 'Give me my clothes.'

'What's the problem? You can take it any time. But will we ever meet again? So is it not better to celebrate now? Don't you want to see me, without a thread around me … more naked than what you see on the billboards? You were fantasising all that and more no, when you were gaping at the girls?'

'Can I make a call?' he asked.

'No!' she was emphatic. 'And let me tell you something: This cell is no more yours. I've been eyeing one like this since long. But what to do … our misers go around with those cheap Nokia ones. But you are great in that aspect too. So I will keep this with me. As a gift. Or as a souvenir if you prefer. It is now my own. Don't tell this to those lousy pimps out there. I know that you won't mind it. Because you love me, right? But you can take the SIM card from it, if you want it.'

He felt like crying. His eyes brimmed, despite his best efforts.

'Che … lost all your stones! Why are you crying? This is for the first time anyone is crying, pleading with me…' she raised her hand to wipe the tears; he spurned it away.

'I need that phone,' he said. 'I cannot go without it. My phone numbers, addresses and notes are all in there.'

He continued, 'You asked me whether it was my first time in this city and I said no. but now I feel I was wrong. This city is totally unknown to me. The roads, the people, the practices … nothing is familiar to me. The "I" standing in front of you now is also a stranger to me. Such an individual was not there in my life till yesterday. I do not know how and why all this happened. Have pity and return at least this phone to me.'

She looked at him with fascination. A miserable beggar pleading for his life.

Then he told her the reason for his coming to city B. He described the city to her as he had seen it 20 years ago. The city then was simple and less complicated. His life too was a straight line without any complexities. Two decades had changed everything. Now I am staring at the future like standing at a promontory of my life looking down into a deep chasm. I'm unable to understand anything. I am standing in front of myself like a confusing crossword puzzle.

She moved closer to him. 'Are you speaking the truth? How could you stand and stare at girls and enjoy the nude posters, in such a state of mind? And now crying like a docile simpleton.' She lifted her hand, swung and slapped him on his cheek. 'Do not cry looking at me. I don't like it.'

~

Raghu took a long time putting on his clothes. He felt as if it was for the first time that he was wearing those clothes. He was sweating profusely.

She unlocked the shutter and stood up straight, looking at him.

'Wait a minute,' she told him. Turning to the table, she took his cell phone and extended it to him. 'Take it. But don't let those boys see this. They won't agree. Anyone who comes here has to abandon all that they have and leave from here as a *sanyasi*; that is our policy. We allow them only a piece of clothing. But in your present state, ok, take the phone. I had thought of giving you my old phone with your SIM. But no, you will curse me. And your wife will question you … so … ok, you can also take the balance of cash in the purse. Enough to meet the auto fare. You should not harbour any hard feelings against me. What can I do? The money withdrawn from the ATM is money with a record, no? It has to be divided among all others. And so what I will get is a small amount. But you don't bother about it.'

She was lost in thought for a moment before raising the shutter. 'I've a feeling that this is not how you should leave this place. That may arouse total hatred against me when you think of me in the future. That should not be. Come closer,' she said in a commanding voice.

He took two steps towards her.

She then proceeded to remove her clothes one by one. She stood fully nude in front of him. 'Don't you want to see?' she asked. He bowed his head in silence. 'Look at me. This is how you should remember me, come on, look here.'

He was thinking about her body. 'Is this girl beautiful? But is this beauty?' Seeing her in the street, sitting together in the pub, walking along with her, her body had attracted him like a magnet. In another situation even a hint of her marble-like body would have fully aroused him. He would have been on fire. But now her standing in front of him like a statue was not having any effect on him. 'Now I'm not I, nor is this body mine. I've entered the body of someone else. An entry into the life of another,' he thought.

'Come closer,' she said. He obeyed her like a puppet.

'Hold me tight.'

His hands extended mechanically and enveloped her. He did not feel anything. It was as if the sensors have been bisected from his skin. She then raised her hands and embraced him. Then she ran her fingers over his neck and his back like a mother to a child.

'You hate me now, no?'

'No,' he said slowly.

'That's a lie.' She released his body and looked at him. 'Didn't I cheat you, rob you?'

'Doesn't matter. I do not know your life,' he said as if chanting a mantra, moving away from her. 'Your childhood, your home, father and mother. Siblings, friends … the way you grew up … I do not know anything. Is it not all these that makes an individual? How can I blame you, not knowing any of these?'

He looked intently at her body, at her beautiful breasts, neck, cheeks, waist, thighs … And when she turned around, he let his eyes roll with total detachment at her buttocks, the back of her neck….

'What are you looking for?' She enquired.

'Marks of torture. I've heard that girls of your profession are often hurt by customers. Burning cigarette marks, which some of them make … Do they hurt you?'

She looked at him for a few minutes in silence. Then she picked up her clothes and put them on languidly. Raising the shutter she said, 'Go.'

'You did not answer me,' he asked her again. 'Those who come to you, do they hurt you?'

'My dear master, all these sound like the dialogues of a movie,' she said laughing out loudly.

The sound of the shutter going down trailed him.

~

Raghu climbed down the spiralling staircase. He did not look back even once. The three youths were very much there, as of earlier, talking incessantly and laughing intermittently. What language were they speaking? There was not even one familiar word, he felt.

As he neared them, one of them shifted and made way for him. That none of them were looking at him seemed to console him. He did not figure in their talk or in their jokes. For them he was not someone who deserved to be noticed at any point of time in life. Maybe they would have considered him a totally new guy had they met him in some other context. He had not made any imprint in their minds.

On the contrary, those three men who were youth-like in appearance, but who would certainly be in their middle age like he was, would always be there in his memories. Their faces would flash past in any given context of his life. Those three unknown men would be the three milestones of his future life. He stole a glance at them as he climbed down the last step; but they just did not bother about him.

Suddenly his phone began to ring. He felt the ringtone reverberating in the silent ambience. Sunanda's number flashed on the screen.

He accepted the call and said softly, 'Hello'.

~

'Hello.'

Someone hit him on his neck before Sunanda's response could reach him. The cell phone slipped out of his hand to the ground. He turned around to see those little men, who till now were totally indifferent to him, rushing towards him with animosity. He bent down to retrieve his phone. He was eager to find out why Sunanda was calling him. But someone pushed him hard before he could reach the phone. He fell down.

Raghu looked at them from the ground. He saw one of the guys pick up the phone, examine it and then put it into his jeans pocket lazily. Fury and rage fumed within him. These men, these pygmies, who do not even reach up to his shoulder, these pimps, they are responsible for everything that has happened. She insulted him through these people; she obliterated his life through them. She could not have behaved with that kind of arrogance and power had it not been for their support. That phone is the last straw of a weak sinking man. That just cannot be given away.

Raghu got up from the ground and walked towards them. He extended his hand for the phone. They had already resumed their seats on the staircase.

'What's it?' asked one of them with the facial expression of a dead person.

'Give me that phone,' Raghu said.

The short guy who had kept the phone in his pocket, spurned him, 'Go! Why are you standing here? Get lost.'

Raghu rushed at him and slapped him, swinging his hand. He had not anticipated that. He fell down the staircase like a ball. Raghu went after him. He tried to wriggle his phone out from the youth's jeans pocket. Two others intervened, blocking him.

'Move,' Raghu shouted. They raised their hands and held him tight.

Raghu tried to loosen their hold but their hands had the strength of steel. He could not get rid of them, however much he tried. An unprecedented courage seemed to envelop him. He made a loud sound. One of the two closed his mouth the very next instant.

The sound of the shutter going up could be heard from the next floor.

~

She shouted from the top of the staircase, 'You sons of Satan, let him go. I'll settle your accounts.'

One of them hissed at her, 'Who does he happen to be of yours? Husband or sister's husband?'

'Son of a pig, he is my father. But what's it for you?'

'You bitch, not worth a rupee, you did not take his phone and now you're delivering lectures?'

She came down a few more steps and shouted at a high pitch, 'I returned it to him knowingly. And what of it? I make money by shedding my clothes. You bastards get drunk from that money only, no?'

'Shut up, you bitch. I will make pieces of you and dump them.'

'For that you will have to be begotten by another father, you rascal.'

When the attention of the three completely shifted to the quarrel with her, Raghu made himself free and moved towards the one who had taken away his cellphone. He had just got up from the ground where Raghu had pushed him. Raghu tried to put his hand into his pocket.

But before he could even touch the phone, he turned against Raghu. Raghu saw the fire of rage and hatred blazing in his eyes. Before Raghu could take evasive action, a sharp weapon had struck him.

Her cry was clearly heard from the top of the stairs, 'Ayyo … Blood.'

That word remained indelible in his mind, 'Blood'.

He had heard it last the previous morning. While waiting for the autorickshaw, after getting out of the bus, Sunanda had mentioned in a low voice, for his ears only, 'Blood'.

Sunanda had called, he now remembered. He had responded with a 'Hello', when her call had come in. but it was snatched away before she could speak again.

His memory too was being snatched away. Somebody running. Someone going up and down the steps. The sounds were fading. Light was failing. His body was folding up....

The spiralling staircase, the pygmies, and the old building with cracking walls were all fading away one by one.

~

Sunanda said, 'It was all my mistake. There was no need for us to come to this town at all. Could've remained back at home. All these investigations and treatments were available there too. Perhaps it would've been better there. Familiar hospitals, doctors, language ... everything. My insistence was the only reason for us to come here.'

Raghu did not say anything. He looked at her face keenly. He could recall her phone call. But they were not able to talk. Why had she called? His eyes scanned the surroundings. Four walls. Four white walls. A small room. He was lying on the bed. Sunanda on a chair nearby. She was talking. Not over the phone; but directly to him. Sitting in front of him.

A bottle of glucose hanging from the stand. Drops dripping from it. A room in the hospital and its four walls.

The image of an old building with its wall full of green moss came into his mind. A spiralling iron staircase. Three short men on the last staircase. And she shouting fiercely from the top of the staircase. Where is she now?

'Blood,' that was what she said last.

Was it not Sunanda who said that? The picture of her leaning on the seat just as he turned and looked from the steps of the bus came into his mind. When was it?

Raghu looked at Sunanda. Doesn't she want to consult the doctor? When will the results of the tests be available?

Sunanda asked softly, 'Do you want to sit up?' He did not answer.

She continued, 'I should not have let you go alone that day. You don't take care anymore. It is as if you are just floating along with the wave. Again it was my fault. Perhaps my selfishness. A longing to be alone. A hope that I talk to myself all alone and that mind will gradually calm down. Did I not compel you to go? But after you left I became worried, thinking that you would be wandering about with your usual carelessness and typical hurry through the streets. I could have accompanied you, I felt. I had problems. Physical disabilities and other issues. But when I realised that you were all alone … images of various types of mishaps rushed into my mind. Suddenly, I wanted to hear your voice. Not because anything had gone wrong. Only for an assurance that everything was ok.'

That was why she had dialed his number. 'You had picked up my call, no? I heard your voice. But that was all. Then the call dropped. And it was always switched off after that. That was a signal for panic. It would've been alright had I not called. But now I had heard you and then it had broken off. I was in total confusion, not knowing what had happened. To whom do I enquire? Whom do I ask for help? Whom do we have in this city for that? We chose this city exactly because nobody here knows us.'

'I tried to keep the world out of bounds. And then the world pushes me out with absolute derision. How easily done, no?'

'You did not come back that night. There has not been a longer night in my life. The anxiety of not knowing what had happened exhausted me. The secretions of my body had come to a stop. Or was it continuing? The truth is that I was not bothered about it anymore. I thought I would go out to the reception and find out. It was then that I understood why you had said that we should not go for such small lodges. The fellow at the reception was dead drunk. He peered at me with suspicion. Asked me whether I stay in that lodge and smiled lewdly. I returned to the room. The whole night I was trying to get you over the phone. Every time it was the same message. I was cursing myself and perhaps you too. Where did you go leaving me all alone? There was nothing I could do. It was late in the night. A weak sick woman—that was all I was.'

'I cried, cursing my helplessness. The previous day's journey, lack of sleep, I was totally exhausted. And at some point of time, I fell asleep. You had not come even when I woke up. The day was brightening. Light mixed with darkness. I woke up again. I pressed your number on the cell phone, invoking all the gods we had abandoned a long time ago.'

'This time it responded. After three or four rings someone picked up. My fingers were trembling. I waited to hear your voice. But there was only silence. I was in a shock not able to get any words out of my mouth. Then gathering all the shreds of energy that remained in my life, I said slowly, "Hello".'

~

'Hello,' a cold scared greeting.

'It was a woman's voice on the other side. I thought I bungled the number. But it was this number that I had called the whole of yesterday. I remained silent in that confusion. Then the same voice from the other side, "Hello, you do not know me. But I know you".'

'Who are you?' I asked. 'This is my husband's number. Who are you?'

'No one,' she said. 'Don't get upset. Are you better now?'

'It is ok,' I said. 'Nothing wrong with me. But…'

'Listen, there was a small incident. Your husband had a small accident. Nothing serious. There is a wound near the shoulder bone. There is some blood-loss. The wound has been stitched. He is in a state of shock. He is sleeping.'

I cried.

'See, there's nothing to worry about. I had a talk with the doctor. She said it was only the after-effect of the blood loss. Nothing more. He can leave the hospital within a day or two.'

'"Where is he?" I asked. She mentioned the name and address of this hospital.'

'"But no need to rush. Finish whatever you have to do and then come. I am here. Will go only after you come. In fact I need to see you. Be brave." She consoled me and cut the call.'

'I dressed in a hurry and got out. The drunkard was still there at the hotel reception, sleeping. It had become bright outside. I could see the streets waking up. I got into an auto and came over. You were in this same condition. Apparently sleeping. The doctor repeatedly said that there was nothing to be worried about. "Just a shock; let him wake up. There is nothing, other than this wound. Luckily it is not very deep." But I was really afraid. All the while I was thinking of it. The guilty feeling that I had sent you away for the sake of my privacy. And then the anxiety as to what would happen next. That is all over now. Now that you have opened your eyes.'

Raghu remained on the bed in the same position, looking at her. That dimly lit room, the pulled-down shutter and the three pygmies marched through his mind again. And then that young girl. Was all of it real?

All of it happened, isn't it? Or even that happened. Sunanda pointed to the bandage as if emphasising all that was real and continued. 'It is not very deep.'

'But you too erred. Perhaps an unnecessary one. Or a blunder. That was not very necessary, no?'

Raghu looked sadly at Sunanda's face.

~

'The examination was just over, the result has not come yet, then why did you withdraw all this money from the ATM? Will anyone wander about with all that money in a totally unfamiliar place? That too all alone. It was really very foolish. That is why I always say that you don't have any presence of mind. You would laugh whenever I say this. Now see what happened. Anyway it was a good lesson. But I'm not convinced that you will not repeat it. You'll get into similar trouble too.'

'But you were lucky this time. Got everything back. What exactly happened? Do you remember? What were you doing in that narrow lane with all that money? Walking through a deserted street with money, phone and a gold chain? Even kids would not behave like this. It turned out to be something like a show for the thieves. This is a big city and naturally, there will be big-time thieves too. They will do anything for money. Now this ended in fisticuffs and an attack with a knife. If it was a really bad time, they would not have hesitated to kill. Ours is a bad world. Very bad.'

'That woman, no she is just a grown up girl. It was she who brought you here. You fell down with the knife strike. She happened to be somewhere nearby. Those thieves, they ran away frightened by the cries. She is indeed brave. Had it been me, I'd have fainted seeing all this.'

'Not just courage, she is a girl full of goodness. See, money, phone, your chain … everything she entrusted to me. She works somewhere nearby. She couldn't stay back till you woke up; she had to go to the office, no? In the confusion and grief I could not even thank her properly.'

'Where is she now?' Raghu asked softly.

Helping him to sit up leaning on a pillow, she said, 'I don't know. Did not get an opportunity to ask. But this has to be said of her, she was like a fairy. She was as beautiful as her mind was.'

'Sita. That is her name, isn't it?' Raghu asked.

'Hey, how do you know that?' Sunanda gaped at him with wonder. 'You knew her before?'

'No,' he said slowly.

'But, oh, that's good. How did you get that name? Were you awake in between?'

'No,' Raghu stared at her and said softly, 'I guessed, that's all.'

That night it rained quite unexpectedly. The lightning which peeped in through the window panes brightened the faded walls. Raghu remained on the bed without sleep, listening to the sound of water falling from the roof of the hospital building.

~

The next day, it was Sunanda's hospital day, Raghu managed to get discharged from the hospital in the morning. The wound was in the process of healing. The doctor had told Raghu, when he insisted, 'I had thought that I'd let you go after two more days. You should take care that there is not much of shaking when travelling by bus. And all medicines are to be taken regularly. And you have to get the wound dressed every day.' Raghu nodded, agreeing to everything she said.

'That would have been better,' Sunanda said, while in a taxi from the clinic. 'After two more days, on complete healing.'

'We have to get the tests results,' Raghu said.

'I'd have gone alone for that. And two more days would not have mattered,' Sunanda became silent looking out.

'Are you afraid?' Raghu asked. She nodded no, even as her eyes became wet. He noticed that her face had become anemic and her eyes were tired. There was a black shadow below her eyelids. She brushed aside strands of oil-less dry hair from her face. He recalled an old photograph of hers. He had got it from her before their wedding to show to his friends. She was like this in that photo. Looking at a distant point, adjusting the hair that the wind had blown on to her face.

'You are beautiful,' he told her in a soft voice, like conveying a secret.

'You have not yet recovered from that shock. That is why you feel like this,' she said without looking at him.

Raghu looked outside. They were on a road with very little traffic. There were puddles of the previous night's rain on the sides. The rain trees were wet and stooping on to the earth.

Looking into her eyes, he told Sunanda, 'Nothing is going to happen, nothing'. He slowly held her hands.

He was touching her knowingly after a very long time. He found those hands unfamiliar. They have thinned. Delicate nerves were visible. They were slightly warm too.

'Nothing will happen,' he repeated. They sat looking out.

The car was entering the outskirts of city B. the high rises were gradually losing their heights.

'Do you remember, the first time we came to this city?' Raghu asked. Sunanda looked at him with sad eyes.

'That was a summer too,' Raghu recalled. 'But it was not this severe. This city used to be cool round the year. A fan was not necessary even during the daytime. That was the reason people came here during the holidays. There were no unending processions of vehicles on the road. They did not huddle on the roads like now, emitting smoke and spreading dust. The footpaths were also not so crowded. The days were brighter! Do you remember, we walked through all these streets then? The big trees spread shade for us. Many things were a first time for us. Big shops, things, spiralling staircases, restaurants. We had many cups of ice-cream with exotic names, sitting in cool lights. I had pushed aside the plate of noodles without even tasting it. I had felt that the noodles resembled earthworms and you made fun of me … no?'

'One day we went to a hill station barely three hours from here. A bright day it was. The bus moved up very slowly. It seemed to stop for a little while at hairpin curves, as if to take a breath and then resumed. Evenly cropped tea plantations spread out like a green sea. We could not see the full expanse of it at one glance. It was cooler out there. We never felt it was summer.'

He continued talking about that trip and the sights in his subdued voice. She grunted, recalling all that. The old city, old time, life, everything came into her mind. Why did they never come back to that place, even though they had liked it so much, they wondered. They lead a very busy life those days. A tense life that did not give them the time to look back and ponder and made them behave like mechanical dolls. The routine, routine jobs, the periods that came regularly every 28 days, the flows, the uninvited loneliness that manifested between them. He talked about all that and about children and love.

Sunanda sat close to him. She too was remembering all that. The last 20 years that passed by.

At some point of time he came back to their last journey. That city, those dear days. They would go to the famous ground in the evening. Walking through the garden, the fallen yellow flowers tickled the feet. Old couples enjoying the cool breeze, children on seesaws and swings. Birds, dear animals. A garden of roses of different colours. Green bushes shaped in the form of birds and animals.

That too was a summer. But a softer, mild sun. Clear sky, clear pictures. They were different human beings. It seemed to be the life of somebody else. It was another city in those days. Or another time, another summer.

~

Helmet, not for Sale

KL 07 AB 321. The motorcycle was covered by a soiled bed sheet. Its handle bar projected out of the cloth-wrap. The young man lifted the sheet very slowly, as if imitating the movements of a magician and hung it on the nearby clothes line. Stepping back, he examined the vehicle as a whole. When he went nearer to the bike and patted the seat, dust which had settled for long, billowed out. He turned to the middle-aged man with a pale smile.

The man didn't make any comments. He just stared at the young man.

He deliberated for some more time and then said, 'Things are not like you think sir. Everything becomes old and stale very fast in these times. If you try selling something you bought yesterday, you'll be lucky if you get half the price. The prices of even new arrivals are at a lower level. Not just that; newer and newer things crowd the market. And after all, old things are old, whether you have used it for a long period or used it for only a day. Who will be ready to buy? These days human beings too are treated in the same manner, no? Some of my friends working in big cities say that people generally take them to be old men! You must remember that they are not yet 30, as of now. All of them bachelors. These days one should be very careful even about closing one's eyes for a moment. The world would have changed by that time.'

He heard the sounds of the auto rickshaw that had brought him there, leaving.

He continued, 'Don't get me wrong, when I say all this sir. Because I'm fully aware of your situation. That's why I came here in person. These days I go personally only for selling large vehicles. It is my employees who deal with two-wheelers. Actually, we are not interested in small vehicles these days. Lot of space is required to store them, no? Last year I had purchased 15 cents of land. You should come and have a look at it now. No space there even for a pinprick. Could have made lakhs, if I had resold the land. But I continue with the sales of used vehicles. I've been in it for years, no? It has become a habit. And it also provides livelihood to quite a few, no? Is it not a big thing?'

He took out a tiny pencil stub and a small diary from his pocket, without waiting for an answer to his question. He turned the pages of the diary hurriedly and noted something on an empty page.

'Look at this,' he continued, displaying his diary. 'This book is full of the market price of vehicles. I record it everyday and preserve it. I can state with certainty that my accounting is far more accurate than anybody else's. Please don't think I'm boasting. This business is something, which I have been doing since long, no? As I said a while ago, these are not old times. Accurate accounting is a necessity of the times. Or you will become out. The new vehicles are totally different from the old ones. How easy things were in the days of Ambassador, Fiat, Bullet or Rajdoot! Now there are hundreds of models and hundreds of varieties! No one can survive without making a detailed study. 'The days of old-time brokers are also over. Then it was the same broker for cattle and cars. The same people would approach with marriage proposals. But those are not done things anymore. Just think for a while, would anyone with my qualifications turn out as a broker in those times?'

The young man tightened his wrists on the handlebar and put the bike on the central stand. The glass of the head light was shattered. The tummy-like fuel tank was apparently intact, but for a slight scrape. KL-07 AB 321 was its number. The number in descending order was easy to remember. The old man recalled spending 1,000 rupees extra for securing that specific number.

'That's yet another difficulty,' the young man said as if reading his mind. 'You might feel that this is a good number. But there is a big problem with this number. Instead, had it been 123, things would have been far more easy. 1..2..3, there is an upward movement in its natural flow. But this 3..2..1, it is going down every step. There is only weariness and fatigue in it. It was a pity that this number was selected. People take notice of all that sir. Had I been consulted, I would not have agreed for choosing this number. But what is the point in thinking about it! What has happened has happened. The price has to be reduced by at least 1,000 for the sake of the number. But, knowing your present circumstances, I will not go to that extent. I had told you over the phone, no, that I am not looking for profit in this deal. I want to settle your account. Even if I incur a loss I will take it in its stride. I'll give up half the interest. I just want the accounts to tally. You know that I gave you the loan merely on the strength of a cheque leaf. I did not press you to pay, even though there was default after the incident. After all, our relationship goes back for long.'

He opened his diary and made one more jotting. He took the bike off the stand, turned the key and kicked. It slowly started after growling for some time.

'Lucky me,' he said. 'It's starting alright. I was worried. Maybe the battery is okay. Is there any other…'

'No chance. It was driven all the way from there. Moreover, the boy next door who works in a workshop examined the bike and confirmed that it is in good condition.'

'Things might look alright now, sir,' the young man suddenly corrected him. 'You see, such a big accident has taken place, and many issues will surface only gradually. That is how it happens. The entire inside would have been shaken up severely. After a while, the nuts and bolts and tightened screws will come loose. Even a total overhauling of the engine may become necessary soon. These machines are similar to the human body. You may have seen thieves who were thrashed by the police when they were youngsters. Their lifeblood would have been sucked out. They might survive because of the natural flourish of youth. But what after that! Ok, let it go. Let's not bring all that into the picture right now.'

He stopped short as if he had come into a firm decision. Then he gathered courage and started off very slowly. 'Take, for example, your own son's case. After he crashed in the accident, nothing seemed to be wrong with him, no? In fact he even stood up. There was not even a scratch on his body. Not a drop of blood was spilled. I am talking about it since I know exactly what had happened. He was taken to the hospital only for confirming that nothing was wrong with him. Some people even argued that it was not necessary. But after a couple of hours passed … I heard that he had vomited and I sensed that things were going wrong. He had banged his head on the road, when he crashed. That is exactly what I'm saying. Similar things happen to vehicles too. The injuries would be inside. Nothing would be visible.'

The old man's face drooped. He looked as if he had viewed a few gruesome canvases.

'Sir, please forgive me,' the young man said. 'I didn't mean to be harsh.'

'It's ok....' The old man looked at him with emotion-drained eyes. The bed sheet on the line was fluttering in the wind.

Neither of them spoke for a while. The mild drawl of the bike which was still in start mode was the only sound that remained.

'So, I hope you are accepting the amount I mentioned on the phone? You must have noticed that I had already foregone half of the interest. And I'm giving up this business of lending money, sir. I don't have time for all this.'

The old man did not speak, but extended his hand and accepted the currency notes, He put the notes in his pocket without bothering to count. The edges of the notes could be seen jutting out of his pocket.

'Please count and verify,' the young man said.

The old man raised his hand and signalled that it is not necessary. The young man wiped his spectacles and put them back on. He then patted the bike as if saying farewell.

He took his diary and replaced it in his pocket. He sat on the bike and waved to the old man.

'Please wait,' the old man said and went into the house. The young man remained on the bike wondering what the old man was up to.

The old man returned after a while with a black-coloured helmet in his hand. He undid its buckle and extended the helmet to the young man. 'Please take this also with you,' he said.

The young man examined it thoroughly and was about to say something.

'Please don't quote a price,' the old man said, not allowing him to speak. 'You should go wearing this. It will suit you.' He stared at the young man's head and took a mental measurement. 'I got this for him, when he was adamant about buying a bike. Just for my mental peace,' his voice faltered. 'That day also I had asked him to wear the helmet. But children being children, they do not always listen to our words.'

The young man could see the old man's eyes brimming.

The young man put on the helmet. He felt suffocated, even though the helmet was a perfect fit for him.

'It is ok, no?' the old man asked him.

The young man tried to say yes, but no sounds came out of him.

~

A Fistful of Mustard Seeds

There was a large crowd of men and women, hands raised and controlling their breath, in the semicircular hall. She felt that those human beings were like huge birds aspiring to fly. At certain rhythmic frenzies of the prayer, many of them were even trying to reach new heights by standing on their toes. All of them were dressed in white. When the entire lot raised their hands, she heard the tender whispers of rustling clothes in the cool breeze.

Guruji was speaking at the big hall of the ashram after quite a long period. He spoke with words as well as with his body. He danced to the accompaniment of musical instruments. He spoke in a subdued feminine voice about the frenzied life of the present times and the interludes human beings lose. He stopped talking in between, and led his followers to *yoga mudras* he had designed. His aura then was that of a great magician, who with his invisible holy stick controlled the inward and outward breathing of many silent human beings.

The hall was dimly lit. Hanging lamps were emitting a dull light as if passing through snow. The delicate tune of a violin emanating from the loudspeakers fixed on the pillars, hovered around as a background score.

Standing silent and with both hands raised high, the Guruji reminded one of a slender bird with a large beak. His face is gleaming, she thought. All those who stood around him in circles also had their eyes closed and hands raised. They were all silent.

Suddenly her cell phone, which was in her handbag, erupted. Its exotic ringtone went on without a pause, piercing the silence in the hall. She was perplexed. It was not possible to leave the hall with the bag. All the doors of the hall were closed, maybe to ensure undisturbed meditation. Confused she fumbled with the zip. Finally she managed to stop the ringtone. She stood up, sensing the antipathy of the crowd rising like a wave. Guruji's address had come to a halt. Her ears tried to conjure up the music that had seemed to engulf the hall, but it had faded out. Other participants, with their hands down, seemed to be drained of everything. She felt that they were all branding her as the accused. She bent her head without a word.

Guruji looked at her calmly and asked, 'You were told that the cell phone had to be entrusted with the reception. Didn't you realise that this was what would happen if the phone suddenly became active?'

She did not have an appropriate answer.

'Someone from outside is trying to contact you.' Guruji's voice filled the hall through the microphone. 'It means that you are not completely inside this hall. Relationships are like strings. They seize you and hold you uncomfortably tight even when they are invisible. It was to avoid such relations, at least for the time being, that phones are not allowed inside the hall.'

That was correct. Those at the reception were collecting cell phones. She had refused to do so deliberately. Perhaps someone, from somewhere, may call. The expectation that some information will come through, still remained. She had never thought that she will be confined to such a space that does not have any contact with the outside world.

An unknown number had flashed on the cell phone screen. 'Who could it be?'

She had come to the ashram early in the morning. And she had presumed that she would be leaving early. Mrs Mehta had given her the firm assurance that all obstacles will vanish on quoting her name. Yet she could not meet Guruji when she reached in the morning. He was not there in the ashram at that time. He would reach in the morning, she was told over the phone the previous evening. 'That is because the flight is delayed,' the middle-aged man with the thick frame told her. 'It need not be a matter of concern, Amma, yours is a three-day course, no? He will certainly reach before that. Probably today afternoon. And he will also be talking to everyone.'

She did not tell him that she was not here to attend the three-day course. She was quite disturbed when he addressed her as 'Amma', despite him being many years senior to her. Maybe this is the custom of the ashram. Maybe she could go back today and come again, after confirming that he is here? She chose this question instead of trying to tell him that he had not come for the course. The middle-aged man looked at her with his smiling eyes. 'See Amma, you are being registered for the three-day course. You have come prepared for that. Then why all this hurry-burry for things that you can't postpone for three days? And moreover, Guruji does not allow any visits through the duration of the course. That is the rule. Now please decide what you want to.' When he once again looked at her with his smile, she wrote down her name and address in the register. She thought that she could leave immediately after meeting Guruji. After all, she stands to lose only the amount collected as the course fee.

She had seen people in the registration queue handing over their cell phones at the reception. That was also a stipulation. Breaking off all contact with the outside world and leading a totally free life, was laid down as a condition in the leaflet. That is just impossible for her to abide by, right now. It is summons from the outside world that one is waiting for. They have ceased to be, is her problem. She got out of the reception area without making any mention of the cell phone in her handbag.

That is what the Guruji is asking now. She fumbled with the phone, hastily switched off the unknown number and looked at Guruji, raising her face. She could not control herself for who knows what reasons. She buried her face into the small towel that was there on the seat along with the round pillow, and burst out crying. All those who till then were staring at her accusingly, withdrew their gaze from her, as if they had committed a crime.

'Don't cry.' Guruji's voice had an unusual boom. 'Because, as I had mentioned in the beginning, crying is not a solution for anything.'

The sobbing under the towel did not stop. Occupying the chair in the centre, Guruji gestured to everyone to take their seats. Sitting on the small beds that looked like baby mats, the rest of the audience cast side glances at her.

Violin tunes had recommenced from the speakers on the pillars.

Guruji slowly stood up. The tip of his long, white-coloured robe was creeping after him on the floor. He was tall and lean. A *rudraksha* garland was wrapped around his neck. His long hair was brown in colour. Eyes that concealed arrows. A vast forehead with wrinkles. Climbing down the small steps, he walked barefoot across the marble floor towards her.

She was struggling to control her sobbing.

Guruji extended his fingers to touch her face and said, 'Suppressed grief is your problem. Tell me, what happened?'

But she couldn't speak. Every time she tried to speak, a wave of sobs would take away her words.

'Please disperse. It is enough for now,' Guruji said to the crowd.

She raised her face in bewilderment and stared at him. 'Is it because of her that he cut short his speech?'

As if reading her mind, Guruji said, nodding his head, 'Don't be upset. I was about to finish anyway. Come and meet me after some time. I'll be there in the outer room.'

Disciples and servants opened the doors and windows. It was summer time. A breeze carrying the warmth of the sun swept through the air-conditioned hall.

'No crying while praying,' Guruji said, gesturing at her to sit on the chair. 'To be factual, there is something wrong in crying, no? Like making a demand for an object? It is children who exploit crying with expertise. That is their way (of getting things done). And our predicament. Grownups like you ought to try to understand yourselves through praying. And not expecting for help from outside.'

She did not sit and instead just stood in front of the cane chair.

'Have you not done basic courses elsewhere?' Guruji asked in low tone.

'No,' she shook her head.

'I guessed as much,' Guruji said. Only those who have completed basics are given admission here. They would have a general idea of such things.'

She remained silent. The growl of the air conditioner was the only sound in the room.

'Okay. If not for the course, what made you come to the ashram? Perhaps you are aware that I do not entertain visitors?'

'I came here only to meet you,' she said in a very low tone. Guruji looked at her intently as if asking what that was for. Her eyes were swollen due to lack of sleep for the last few days.

'Mrs Mehta advised me to meet you, Swamiji…' she fumbled, not quite sure of herself.

'Mrs Mehta?' Guruji tried to recall, 'Oh … Sarala Behen, you mean the colonel's wife?'

'Mm!' her eyes became wet. 'She suggested that perhaps you may be able to help…'

'Sarala Behen has misunderstood me; despite her knowing me since long. As I said before, I don't think anyone from outside can be of any help to you,' Guruji smiled. 'Perhaps I may be able to point out a solution that is very much there in you, that is all. Guruji repeated it like a mantra, 'that's all.'

Neither of them spoke for a while. She stood inert, her gaze alternating between the three Tibetan wall hangings.

'But you have not told me what do you want me to do?' Guruji said snapping his long fingers.

She was on the verge of tears. She tried to cover her face with the *pallu* of her sari. Guruji continued to watch her with profound calmness.

A servant dressed in white, walked in with glasses and a bottle of water. He kept them on the table and exited in absolute silence. Everyone in the ashram was dressed in white. A life discarding colours. Or as Mrs Mehta always says, 'A life imbibing all colours'.

'My son…' She commenced, but words failed her.

'Tell me, what happened to your son?' Guruji tried to compose a *mudra* with his fingers.

'My son. He is missing…' she said that much, but couldn't control herself anymore. She sobbed, trying to hide her face.

'Please sit down,' Guruji stood up and addressed her. 'I just don't like anyone standing in front of me like this.'

She pulled up the chair and sat on it slowly, with downcast eyes.

'How long since your son has gone missing?' Guruji asked.

'It was on the 30th. Today, as of today it is full five days,' she said, calculating in her mind.

'He is studying, no? In which class?'

'Just completing four years. He attends the nursery school.'

'Did he go missing from there?'

'No.'

'Then?'

'A bit far away, in a train.'

'Where did it happen?' she felt that Guruji was trying to assess her.

'After Kharagpore. We were going to Calcutta.'

'When you say "we", your husband was with you?'

'There was … a friend. A colleague.'

'Oh, I didn't ask, where are you working?'

'In the Microbiology department of the University. In a medical project.'

Neither of them spoke for a while.

'Where is your husband?' Guruji asked, as if he had recalled something.

'He is out of India. In an oil rig. Presently at the outer sea of an island in the Pacific.

'The islands in the Pacific ocean,' Guruji repeated without any specific reason, 'I had flown over them only a few days ago.'

'We were going for the collection of a specimen,' she recalled. 'That was a requirement for the completion of Richie's research.'

'So this Richie is your friend?' Guruji guessed. 'Where is he now?'

'No idea…' She resumed crying. 'I don't know where he is.'

'Your son and him. Both of them became untraceable at the same time?'

'Together ... No. First my son; then Richie went in search of him.'

'You did not inform the police?' Guruji asked looking at her with his piercing eyes.

'I ... I do not know anything, Guruji. My son ... I'm scared.'

'Daughter!' He called her in a very low voice. It was as if he was addressing himself. 'Is it that you have not informed any of these things to your husband?'

'Once he comes to know of this...' her face went down with fear.

'How can you keep it from him? Certainly, he must have known that you were going to Calcutta with the child?

'We don't contact each other frequently these days.'

'Any problems between you two?

She merely nodded.

'So, no phone calls?'

'Yes. Once in a while he calls our son. But these days I've not been attending the calls from his number.

'Do you mean that there have not been any calls after your son went missing?'

'No. He had called yesterday.'

'Then?'

'I didn't take the call. By the time he called again, I had switched off the phone. I talked to Mrs Mehta after that. She suggested that maybe you can help me.'

'You mean to say that Sarala Behen did not suggest informing the police? Though she is the wife of a military officer?'

'Madam did not ask me anything about it, Guruji.'

'Whatever it be, not informing the police is not correct. Let them enquire. At least your friend, that fellow Richie is to be enquired about. Is he a Malayalee?'

'Richie is a foreigner. A guy who has come from Nigeria on a student's exchange programme. A nigger,' she said.

'Black,' Guruji corrected her. 'That means their embassy also will have to be informed.'

'My son … my son … Guruji please tell me, when will I get him back,' she looked at him sobbing.

Guruji could feel a strange kind of helplessness encircling him. What is happening? Are the people mistaking *sanyasin*s to be astrologers?

'In fact Richie does not like children. I've never seen him mollycoddle a child.' She continued, looking at Guruji. 'To be honest, which child will like him? Richie is a giant of a man, fat and tall with thick lips. A chain smoker. He is not even 30, but practically bald. He wears a tee-shirt with small sleeves, so that one can see the tattoo of a dragon on his arms. I don't know how to describe him? Like Lothar in Mandrake comics. In the beginning I was afraid even to talk to him.'

Guruji tried to draw a picture of Richie on his mental canvas.

'Richie used to avoid me when I told him that the child is to be picked up from school. He has told me that he can't stand children. Not even their mischief, cries and childish babbling. He can't stand them. So he was not interested in taking the child to Calcutta along with us. As for me, I was apprehensive about entrusting him with anyone else.' She stopped for a while and looked at Guruji. He had been listening to her narration without any expressions.

'That was his childhood. He was born in a ghetto. He had no idea of who his father was. Richie once told me that his mother died of AIDS. Richie always used to say that no one has any right to beget children and abandon them to a hellish life.'

'Africa confuses us even now.' Guruji said. 'I'm still afraid of going there. Have you seen the elephant-ear like map of Africa?'

She did not come up with an answer for that. Maps no more exist in my memories, she felt.

'But the child took to Richie in the very first moments in the train. That was the surprise. I had not seen him playing with such warmth along with anyone till then.'

'Tiny tots can love without any preconceived notions,' Guruji said.

'Now I feel that Richie was making use of it. Perhaps to impress me,' she stopped suddenly.

Guruji was not alarmed. He merely looked at her without making any attempt to question her.

'On the second day we changed over into Coromandel Express from Chennai. The coach we were in was not very crowded. Elderly people wrapped in woollen blankets were our co-passengers. They were sleeping throughout. They did not hide their protest whenever my son made any loud sounds. Richie seemed to enjoy the whole show. The child played with Richie climbing over his fat body. He persuaded Richie to be his elephant.'

'Richie told me once that other kids never included him in their games when he was a kid. They were afraid that he may be infected with HIV. The priests who had adopted him found the situation quite murky. They must have felt bad that a boy who was good in studies was being isolated.'

The servant who had put in an appearance earlier on, came with a cup of tea for her.

'He would not talk to me in the beginning. His habits were weird. He enjoyed tormenting half-dead insects like lizards, rats etc., in the lab. I did not like this habit of his at all. In fact our first conversation was a quarrel about this.'

Outside someone was beckoning another person very loudly. Guruji's face turned in that direction for a while.

'"None of you can ever imagine the life in a ghetto," Richie told me. "No one has the macabre imagination required for that." He said he had grown up physically alright, but he claimed that his mind was still bogged down in the slush.'

'Between you and him…?' Guruji asked her, gesturing at her to drink her tea.

'Yes,' she hesitated for a moment, yet continued. 'I had just sent the divorce notice. There were many situations when we two were alone in the lab. I used to share with Richie the history of the faltering relationship with my husband.'

'But he never, not even once, attempted to comment on it. When I cried, unable to control my grief, his arms would encircle me in a hug. I would feel as if I was taking refuge under a dark cloud seeking its shade in the hot sun.'

'He has come to my flat several times. Many times even at night, after confirming over the phone that my son has slept. I lay like an exhausted prey under his massive body. That black body smelled of tobacco. I was even delighted in being shattered under him. Naturally people started talking. A black man frequenting my apartment was noticed by all others. My acquaintances started calling me over the phone. There was no shortage of advice too … but I ignored all of it. I don't know why, I had a feeling of adventure all the while. I was happy thinking that I was having my own revenge against my husband.'

The tea was not sweet enough. It was not very warm too. She finished it in a gulp.

'What happened at Kharagpore?' Guruji asked.

'At Kharagpore…' She stopped for a while and tried to recollect. 'It was almost noon. The train was to be at the station for quite some time. Many passengers got out of the coach and loitered on the platform. There was a flurry of trains on the other platforms. I was nourishing a headache since the morning.

I went up on my berth and covered myself completely. It was then that my son demanded ice cream. I tried to convince him that he should not have ice cream from such shops. But he was adamant. And this was how Richie went out along with him.'

'I don't know how long I lay down on the berth. It was as if I was sleeping.'

'I heard Richie's voice, when the train started. He was teasing me in a high-pitched voice. So I did not bother about my son. I assumed him to be with Richie. I was aware of the train gathering speed.'

'"What do you want for lunch?" Richie woke me up by patting me gently.'

'Something light will do for me. I am not the least hungry,' I said.

'"What about him? He had told me in the morning that he wanted non-veg," Richie smiled.'

'You ask him directly. His food habits have become a problem now, because of you,' I said.

'"What have I done? Let him say what he wants. And you always make him sleep by your side, no?" Richie teased me.'

'Who?' I sprang up. He was with you, no?'

'"Now don't joke, ok?" Richie said. "Didn't I see him boarding the train with the ice cream cup?"'

'You didn't get in with him?

'"I stayed on the platform for a smoke. If I were to smoke sitting in the coach, you would readily hand me over to the police, no?", he said.'

'I jumped out of the berth. Sharply looking at his face, I asked him: "Richie, now don't play games. Where is Arun?"'

'"Didn't I tell you? I saw him rushing to you," he replied.'

'Oh I can't bear this…' I could sense a tremor enveloping me from top to bottom. 'He didn't come here.'

'"Calm down! He will be here. I saw him getting into the train," he protested.'

'I do not want to hear any explanations. I want to see him right now.'

'I was agitated seeing Richie standing rooted despite my words. He did not like children. Then why did he befriend my son? I recalled what he used to say about his own childhood. I remembered with terror how he used to derive pleasure poking the reptiles in the lab with his smouldering cigarettes.'

'Standing like a stone! Go and get him you son of a bitch!'

'Noticing that the old men around us were becoming curious, Richie left the compartment. I saw his huge body swaying along with the coaches as he crossed the vestibule.'

'The train hurried along without stopping anywhere. Too tired and weary, I slumped on the seat, my face drooping. Those around me eating and talking—I was not seeing them. I felt that every moment Richie was away, was as extended as an era.'

'Richie came back, I do not know when. His face was pale.'

'"Let's get down at the next station and go back," Richie said, "most probably he is still there at Kharagpore platform."'

'I couldn't control my tears. Richie was in absolute confusion, not knowing what to tell me. We got down from the train at the next station, a small affair.'

'You ought to have filed a complaint there itself,' Guruji said.

'I tried to do it,' she said. 'It was Richie who said, "Let's wait".'

'Why?'

'That was what I couldn't understand. On persuasion, he confessed that there was some problem with his visa. A police case could lead to complications. Moreover, he said he was sure we would get back my child without police intervention.'

'As a mother, you ought to have given a complaint.'

'I too was desirous of getting him back without a case and police. Because my husband was not aware of this journey with our son. I had not told him about it. That morning he had called our son and he had told his father that he was going to his mother's house. He must have believed that. Occasionally we used to go to my house by train.'

'That night we stayed at a hotel near the station. In two rooms. I did not agree with his suggestion of one room. By that time I hated even seeing him. And also…'

'And also?'

'And also I wanted to cry, all alone,' she mumbled feebly, recalling Guruji's words about crying not being a remedy for anything.

'Where did you search subsequently?' Guruji asked her, observing that she was about to cry again.

'Next morning Richie was not there in his room. He had left a message at the reception counter.'

'What did it say?'

'He asked me to go home. That he was searching for my son. It is my son who is missing and how is it going to affect him? I guessed that he would have gone to Calcutta for collecting his specimen. Selfish pig. His play acting and laughter … I realised that I've been swindled.'

'But why curse Richie for your son's disappearance? It was not deliberate, no?'

'I do not know Swamiji … But he ought to have been at my side, no? Will any mother go away leaving her son wherever he is? Moreover, whenever I call Richie I get the message that the phone is switched off.'

'So that was why you returned?'

'What else can I do? What can I do there? Unknown land and unknown people and me all alone.'

Guruji covered his face with his palm and was lost in thought for a while.

'I'm terrified about my son, Guruji. What if something happens to him?'

'Be brave,' Guruji said in a low tone.

'Sometimes, sometimes, beggars getting hold of him…'

'Be calm,' Guruji said. 'There was a call for you during the speech. Who was it?'

'Somebody! I do not know that number.'

'Sarala Behen, does she know all these happenings?'

'Not all. The child is missing, is the only thing I've told her. She doesn't know about Richie.'

'Did you call Richie today?'

'Yes. I keep on calling him. He has switched off his cell. I should not have trusted him.'

Guruji unlocked his palms from his face and concentrated his eyes on her face: 'What I would say…'

She raised her eyes towards him.

'What I would say is…' Guruji continued, 'You should inform everything to your husband at the earliest. He should not be left ignorant of all this.'

'I'm scared…'

'There are things in life that have to be faced. There is no point in evading them. If not today, then tomorrow…'

'Swami you please tell me what will happen to my son…?'

Guruji maintained silence for a moment, perhaps searching for words. He felt that the air conditioner was growling too much. He turned around and saw a Tibetan picture of the praying Buddha on the wall...

'Your grief is your son. There are ever so many mothers in such a condition! I find a great similarity with another story,' he said, 'You may have heard of the story of the young woman who went to Lord Buddha to retrieve her baby from death? He asked her to bring him a fistful of mustard seeds,' Guruji paused.

'She burst out crying and stopped Guruji, 'No Guruji, I too have heard that story. But in that story, the baby…'

Guruji stood up and patted her shoulder, 'Be calm,' he repeated. He felt it was untimely of him to have reminded her of that story. Now she was crying uncontrollably.

'I have only a few techniques with me.' There was a tinge of frustration in his words, she felt. 'A few exercises using yoga, certain breathing and relaxation techniques. But I could suggest remedies for many things. Perhaps remedies that everyone is aware of, but which have to be located from one's own life. Now you have brought your life itself to me, as if it is a big question mark. What advice can I possibly give you? We can't console each other in certain matters. Nor can we suggest remedies. The reason is simple: there are no remedies for them.' By this time, Guruji had commenced walking up and down.

'Especially family relations. What awareness do you expect from me regarding that?' Neither of them spoke for a while. Guruji signaled to a bearer and asked to him bring something cool. 'Cool drinks are better when the body gets warm.'

Time was creeping away slowly.

'Perhaps, perhaps…' Guruji stopped for a moment and said: 'Let's console ourselves that such things will not happen…'

'What do you mean, Guruji?' she asked rising from her chair. She caught hold of his lean body and shook him hard like one possessed and shouted: 'Tell me when I will get back my baby. I came seeking you only for that. Please do not send me away.'

Guruji very slowly loosened her fingers. He touched the *rudraksha* coils around his neck with his long fingers and said, 'It is very hot outside. I have asked for something cool. Please have it before you leave.'

But she did not stay back. While walking towards the parking area, she felt as if the bag hanging on her shoulder was as heavy as as a dead body.

Descent. She drove slowly through the circling mountain tracks with lots of sharp curves. The sun was very hot outside. Parched heaps of dry stones lined the road. A climate that did not allow even grass to sprout. After going down for some time, she turned around and looked back. She could see the golden dome of the ashram glistening in the sun. 'Why did I come to meet Guruji?' she wondered. Mrs Mehta had said that meeting Guruji provides relief for everyone. Instead, the story he narrated today, the story of mustard seeds was smouldering within her like limestone.

'I should not have come to the ashram,' she felt. 'Perhaps what guruji said was right. Remedies, may have to be found out by oneself. Maybe no one can be of help to anyone. Or maybe there are no remedies for certain things. Questions that do not have answers. Like orphan calls that have no response.'

The traffic increased as she descended from the mountains to the plains. Panting vehicles came to a halt at traffic signals. She was trying hard not to think. She was driving like a machine, deliberately taking in only the vehicle right in front, with her full attention on the smoke from its exhaust.

The city was getting closer. The traffic was much more than usual.

She had to wait in the queue at every point. She switched off the engine, when the traffic was reduced to moving in a one-way direction by the police.

While stranded in the traffic, her cell phone began ringing in her hand bag. 'Must be Mrs Mehta. Will she ask her to stay back at the ashram? Mrs Mehta was a blind follower of Swamiji. Should she accept the call?'

She was startled seeing the number that was flashing on the phone screen—Richie. Allowing the phone to ring for some time, she lifted it to her ear.

Nothing was audible.

'Hello, hello.'

No sound. She could not bear her anger and grief.

'You bastard, don't play with me,' she shouted.

No response from the other end. 'What is it that he is trying to tell? Or has he switched off?'

Then she heard a weak cry as if from the borders of the earth. And then a call 'Amma,' from the phone. Her hand holding the phone was shivering uncontrollably. She noticed that the vehicle just ahead had started moving.

She tried to recall the name of that young woman who was asked to fetch a fistful of mustard seeds by the Buddha, as she was turning the ignition key.

~